*Grace
and
Glorie*

GRACE
AND
GLORIE

A Play in Two Acts

BY
TOM ZIEGLER

The Fireside Theatre
Garden City, New York

ISBN 1-56865-272-0

Printed in the United States of America

Tom Ziegler's play *Grace and Glorie* ran Off Broadway at the Laura Pels Theatre and starred Estelle Parsons and Lucie Arnaz. The play was produced previously at the Dorset Theatre Festival where it was selected by the audience as the best play of the season.

His play, *Small Sacrifices*, was a winner of Mill Mountain Theater's "Norfolk Southern New Play Competition" and was presented in the theater's "Festival of New Plays."

His musical, *Glory Bound*, written with Red Clay Ramblers, Jack Herrick, opened to rave reviews at Lime Kiln Theater in Virginia in 1995 and was revived again in 1996 due to popular demand. *Glory Bound* was awarded a developmental grant by the National Endowment for the Arts.

His play *Home Games* opened the Off Broadway season at The Hudson Guild Theatre in 1989 and was directed by Roderick Cook. The play premiered at The American Stage Company in Teaneck, New Jersey earlier that year. *Home Games* has been published by Samuel French and continues to be performed throughout the United States.

Other plays include *The Ninth Step* produced in New York at the Riverwest Theatre also directed by Roderick Cook. *The Last Resort* was produced at the Triangle Theatre in New York City, directed by William Cantler. *The Body Shop* and *Weeds* were produced by the Theatre Department at Washington and Lee University in Lexington. Other projects include an adaptation of Luigi Pirandello's *Six Characters in Search of an Author*. The book and lyrics of a touring comedia musical, *The Lovers of Verona*. His one-act, *Making Ends Meet*, was a winner of the national contest sponsored by the Little Theatre of Alexandria. The play went on to win best original one act in the Northern Virginia Theatre Alliance Competition. His one-act play, *Jesus and Isaac*, won the Congregation Emanu El competition in Houston in 1988 and was revived there again in 1994.

Mr. Ziegler won The Virginia Playwriting Fellowship in 1990 and again in 1993.

The author serves as Playwright in Residence by the MJT Productions of New York City and is a Professor at Washington and Lee University in Lexington, Virginia where he teaches playwriting and scene design.

Dedicated to the memory of
Richard Coyne

Originally produced at the Laura Pels Theatre at the Roundabout in New York City by:
    Edgar Lansbury, Everett King and Dennis J. Grimaldi
    by arrangement with Ted Story
    Associate Producers were Ashley/Bernstein
    Gloria Muzio was the Director

Scenery was designed by Edward Gianfrancesco
Lighting by Brian Nason
Costumes by Robert Mackintoch
Sound by John Gromada
Production Stage Manager was Alan Fox

CAST

GRACE .... Estelle Parsons
GLORIE .... Lucie Arnaz

(Originally presented in a joint production by Theatre Virginia and ShenanArts and later at The Dorset Theatre Festival.

The play received a workshop reading at the Shenandoah International Playwrights Retreat, Robert Graham Small, director.

CAST OF CHARACTERS

GRACE STILES: ninety year old country woman.
GLORIA WHITMORE: late thirties, early forties. A New Yorker.

SYNOPSIS OF SCENES

The entire action takes place in Grace's cottage located in the Blue
Ridge Mountains of Virginia one recent fall.

ACT ONE

Scene 1: A Monday afternoon.
Scene 2: Early the next morning.
Scene 3: Late the following Friday.

ACT TWO

Scene 1: Late Saturday morning.
Scene 2: Early evening that same day.

THE SETTING

A primitive one-room cottage that has been, over the years, "modernized" several times. The place has the feeling that someone has hastily moved in recently. Every corner contains stacks of boxes, household items, old furniture.

A simple kitchen to the right is dominated by a large wood cook stove. The area is furnished with a sink with a hand pump, shelves, an old chrome dinette set, old and rusted refrigerator. The walls on this side of the cabin are made of logs, a sturdy remnant of the original structure. There is a door leading to the back porch.

Near the center is a huge antique bed.

In a "newer" section on the left is one door leading outside to a front porch and another door leading into a small bathroom. Along the wall sits a bureau on top of which is an old television.

Any other available space is *filled* with sewing projects: quilts, rugs, bags of rags, stacks upon stacks of decorative items in various stages of completion. Although most things in the cabin are old, from another time, there are enough items that clearly remind us that the play is happening now. Every attempt must be made to fight the impulse to infuse the setting with country charm.

Three old-time hymns are referred to during the play: "Throw Out the Lifeline" by E. S. Ufford; "Where He Leads Me" by E. W. Blandly; and "Close To Thee" by Fanny J. Crosby.

ACT
ONE

ACT I

Scene 1

We are listening to the sweet sounds of a country farm. Birds chirping, bugs buzzing, occasionally a dog barking in the distance, a chicken clucking. As the house lights dim, the pleasant rural sounds give way to the angry din of heavy earth-moving equipment: bulldozers, graders, trucks. After a moment we hear the voice of a radio disk jockey rising out of the tumult, a woman with a distinct "country" sound.

RADIO VOICE: Comin' up on top of the hour here's one takes me way back. And I'm sure it'll take you way back, too. The Good News Quartet remindin' us that even on a pretty fall day like this we shouldn't forget to— "Throw Out the Lifeline."

QUARTET (*singing*):   THROW OUT THE LIFELINE,
THROW OUT THE LIFELINE,
SOMEONE IS DRIFTING AWAY!
THROW OUT THE LIFELINE, THROW OUT THE LIFELINE,
SOMEONE IS SINKING TODAY!

(*As the quartet belts out the hymn, the lights reveal mid afternoon in the cottage. Grace is in bed under several quilts. She wears a pair of headphones which are attached to a Walkman. From outside we continue to hear the rumble of the heavy earth-moving equipment under the music*)

QUARTET: THROW OUT THE LIFELINE WITH HAND QUICK AND STRONG . . .

3

GRACE (*joining the Quartet*): . . . WHY DO YOU
  TARRY . . .
(*There is a knock on the front door*)
WHY LINGER SO LONG.
(*Another knock, louder*)
SEE! SHE IS SINKING; O HASTEN TODAY . . .

GLORIA (*off, shouting*): Mrs. Stiles?

GRACE: . . . AND OUT WITH THE LIFE-BOAT . . .

GLORIA: Mrs. Grace Stiles?

GRACE: AWAY, THEN AWAY!

GLORIA: Hello! May I come in?

(*Gloria opens the door cautiously. Steps in. She's attractive, dressed in a conservative, expensive suit. She carries a leather attaché case. The rumble of the machinery swells until Gloria closes the door*)

GLORIA: Mrs.—

GRACE (*eyes closed*): THROW OUT THE LIFELINE!

GLORIA: Excuse me, I—

GRACE: THROW OUT THE LIFELINE!

GLORIA: The door was unlocked and I—

GRACE: SOMEONE IS DRIFTIN' AWAY.

GLORIA: Mrs. Stiles?

GRACE: THROW OUT THE LIFELINE! THROW
   OUT THE LIFELINE!
(*Gloria slowly approaches the bed. Grace finishes the song
with a flourish*)
SOME-ONE IS SINK-IN' TO-DAY!
(*Gloria touches Grace's shoulder*)
Oh!

GLORIA: I'm sorry I startled you, Mrs. Stiles. I did knock.
   (*As she talks her voice steadily rises in volume. Grace just
   stares*) I've just come from the hospital. Your doctor told
   me he sent you home this morning. How are you doing?
   You know when they told me you lived up in the mountains I didn't fully appreciate . . . I mean the roads. I
   wasn't sure my car—

(*The machinery roars outside*)

GRACE: Honey, I can see your lips movin' so I know
   you're talking, but I can't hear a blessed word you're
   sayin'! And I ain't gone deaf, if that's what you're thinkin'!
   It's this thing here . . . (*She holds up the walkman*) I was
   hoping me and the Good News Quartet could drown out
   that confoundin' racket!

GLORIA: Here, let me help you with—

GRACE (*snapping*):   I can do it!

GLORIA: Hi. I'm Gloria Whitmore. (*Waiting for some rec-
   ognition, getting none*) You probably don't remember, but
   we met briefly at the hospital last week.

GRACE: I remember. Wha'cha think, I'm senile?

GLORIA: No, of course not.

GRACE: Probably think I'm a little dotty, too, ol' prune like me wearing one of these things. Wasn't none o' my doin'. It was that Bernice. Bernice Wallace? (*Gloria shakes her head*) My roommate there in the hospital. You met her last week, or don't you remember!

GLORIA: Yes, of course.

GRACE: She died yesterday.

GLORIA: I didn't know. I'm sorry.

GRACE: Why? She was eighty-seven years old. Me, I'm ninety.

GLORIA: Yes, I know. Mrs. Stiles, is there anyone here with you?

GRACE: I do believe you are.

GLORIA: No, I mean is your grandson here?

GRACE: Roy? He went back to work.

GLORIA: And left you here all alone?

GRACE: He'll be back this evenin'. You need to talk to Roy?

GLORIA: You should have someone here with you.

GRACE: What for?

GLORIA: What— To care for you.

GRACE: Roy takes care of me. Cuts my fire wood, fetches me things from the I.G.A.

GLORIA: I'm sure Roy's very devoted, but what I—

GRACE: Wouldn't go so far as to say he was "devoted." I gotta pay him. Roy don't do nothin' for free. Listen, just go back down the highway to Ernie's Texaco. That's where he works.

GLORIA: I'm not here to talk to Roy, Mrs. Stiles, I'm here to see you. When you left the hospital this morning you forgot your medication. Here. (*Taking a package from her bag*) An aide found this in your room.

GRACE: You must think I'm a mighty forgetful ol' lady! Well, I'm not! Told the doctor I didn't want none o' that stuff. Nurse, too. Didn't they tell you?

GLORIA: Yes, they did, but—

GRACE: Then why on earth did you drive all the way out here?

GLORIA: Mrs. Stiles, I— I'm— May I sit down?

GRACE: Now you listen to me! I've been through this with all you hospital people fifty times! You people and your drugs. Now I've been doin' it your way for mor'n a year now, and all I can say is, enough's enough!

7

GLORIA: May I sit down?!

GRACE: Honey, I ain't the Queen o' England. You want to sit, sit!

GLORIA: Thank you! (*A breath*) I'm a volunteer with an organization—we're affiliated with Valley General—it's called Hospice. Your doctor said he told you all about us.

GRACE: Did he? Well, he might of. But he was one of them city-bred Yankees could talk a whole lot faster than I could listen.

GLORIA: Didn't he give you some literature that explains our—

GRACE: Some what?

GLORIA (*taking papers from her bag*):   A booklet, some papers, an agreement for you to sign.

GRACE: You're not from 'round here, are you?

GLORIA: Pardon me? Oh. No. I guess I'm a—"city-bred Yankee," too.

GRACE: Listen, honey, I don't mean to be unfriendly, but whatever it is you're sellin', I'm sure I'm way past needin' it. (*Picking up her earphones*)

GLORIA (*going to her briefcase*):   Did you have lunch?

GRACE: What?

GLORIA: I found out you didn't touch your breakfast at the hospital this morning, so I went ahead and packed this thermos of chicken soup. I have fresh biscuits, butter. You know one of the services Hospice provides—

GRACE: I'm not hungry.

GLORIA: Sure you are.

GRACE: TOLD YOU I'M NOT HUNGRY!

GLORIA: You know, maybe it *would* help if I talked to your grandson.

GRACE: Why? Roy don't understand you people no better'n me.

GLORIA: May I use your phone?

GRACE: Sure. It's over there. (*Grace lets Gloria go to the phone, pick it up, start to dial*) Don't work, though. (*Gloria puts the receiver to her ear*) One of them Caterpillar tractors knocked down the line.

GLORIA: I don't believe this! You're out here all alone in the middle of nowhere without a phone? What would you do if you needed help?

GRACE: What I always do. Pray to the good Lord.

GLORIA: Yes. Of course. Then I guess I'll have to drive down and talk to Roy. Ernie's Texaco, right?

GRACE: I really wish you wouldn't bother Roy.

GLORIA: They are going to fix your phone?

GRACE: They're runnin' a whole new cable up from the highway. Said it'd take least two weeks.

GLORIA: Two weeks! But— I'll see about your phone when I get back to town.

GRACE: Don't trouble yourself. Bad enough you had to drive all the way up here for nothin'.

GLORIA: That's all right. Your doctor warned me I'd be driving all the way up here for nothing. At least let me find someone to stay with you. Maybe someone from your church.

GRACE: Don't go to church. Ain't been in one for mor'n fifty years!

GLORIA (picking up her bag): I see. I'll go talk to Roy, then tomorrow morning I'll check back—

GRACE (slight panic): Tomorrow?

GLORIA: What is it?

GRACE: Nothin'. You go along. I'll just . . . get back to The Good News Quartet.

GLORIA: You're sure?

GRACE: I'll be fine. (Gloria turns to go) This walk-man thing! I told you it was all Bernice's doin'! She didn't like me playin' the Gospel station on my radio. "Holy roller

music," that's what she called it. "Holy roller music." So
one day a nurse shows up with this thing. Wants to put it
on my ears. Told her she'll have to wait 'til I die first. But
she kept insistin' and I kept sayin' no 'til Bernice finally
hollers, "Grace, put the damn thing on your ears and shut
the hell up!" You can probably tell Bernice was a heathen.
Said only "fools" believed in God. Fools. Course, like I
said, Bernice died yesterday. Closed her eyes to take a
nap and never opened 'em up again. I was just thinkin'.
Be'cha anything Bernice Wallace believes in God now!

GLORIA: I'm sure she does. Well, I'll be—

GRACE: And bossy. Why I never met a woman bossy as
Bernice Wallace. 'Specially to them nurses. Me, I hated to
bother 'em. Like this morning when I woke up? I had to
make water so bad thought I was goin' to bust. Bernice
could always tell when I had to go. She'd say, "Grace, why
you jumpin 'round like that? You got to pee?" That's how
she said it. "You got to *pee*, Grace?" 'Fore I could even
answer she'd start hollerin' 'till every nurse on the floor
come runnin'.

GLORIA (*finally realizing the problem*):   Mrs. Stiles . . . ?

GRACE: But, like I said, this morning Bernice wasn't
there no more! Ornery old woman went and died on me!
Why, I'll bet the good Lord slaps a "Walk Man" on her
heathen ears and makes her listen to "holy roller music"
for all eternity!

GLORIA: Mrs. Stiles, do you have to go to the bathroom?

GRACE: YES I HAVE TO GO TO THE BATHROOM! GOOD GRAVY WOMAN, I'VE BEEN TRYIN' ALL DAY TO GET SOMEONE TO—

GLORIA: You haven't been to the bathroom since you woke up this morning? (*Grace shakes her head*) Mrs. Stiles, it's the middle of the afternoon!

GRACE: BELIEVE ME, HONEY, I KNOW WHAT TIME IT IS!

GLORIA: Where are your slippers?

GRACE: There in my bag. I tried to say something to them nurses but they was so busy, then Roy was in such a hurry to get back to work. I've been fine, really. Least 'til The Good News Quartet started singin' "Throw Out The Life Line!" That's when I thought my boat was really gonna sink! (*Gloria tries to help Grace up*) Oh.

GLORIA: You're in pain.

GRACE: Please, let me lie back down. (*Gloria eases her back*)

GLORIA: But what are we going to do about—

GRACE: I'll just hold it.

GLORIA: Hold it? Don't be silly!

GRACE: Honey, I grew up the youngest of *thirteen* kids. And we had only one outhouse. One. Why I got so I could hold my water for a week standin' in front of Ruby Falls.

GLORIA: I don't suppose you have a bed pan? (*Taking out her notebook and writing in it*) It's so stupid of me. Why didn't I think to bring one.

GRACE: Now why should you bring a bed pan? I mean it's not exactly the kind of thing people come callin' with.

GLORIA: Let me look in the kitchen, there has to be something—

GRACE: The kitchen? I really don't—

GLORIA: Does Roy live here with you?

GRACE: Roy? Goodness no. This here, this is the "granny cottage." My husband fixed it up for his mamma to live in. After his daddy died? Put in the bathroom over there. Really just a glorified outhouse. Nothin' in there but a toilet and a tin tub. Course Mr. Stiles' mamma only slept down here. Spent the whole day up at the "Big House" with me. (*Gloria goes to a box of dishes*) So wha'cha doin' here anyway? In Virginia I mean. You just visitin'?

GLORIA: My husband and I moved here from New York City in the spring. Peter's joined a law firm in town.

GRACE: Oh, that's where I got my china packed up.

GLORIA: I can see that.

GRACE: You're not gonna find nothin' in there.

GLORIA (*holding up a squat, oval china bowl*): How about this?

GRACE: That's a soup tureen. Belonged to my husband's mother.

GLORIA: Sentimental value, is that it?

GRACE: Wouldn't say the sentiment had much value. Her name was Gabriella. Gabriella Stiles. Lived with us nineteen years.

GLORIA: I see.

GRACE: Yes. Know how some years go by quick, some slow? I'm tellin' you, that was a string of nineteen of the slowest years of my life.

GLORIA: This does have the right shape.

GRACE: Does, doesn't it? No, no, we couldn't. Put it back.

GLORIA: Mrs. Stiles, I know I shouldn't say this, but if I had the opportunity to "pee" in *my* mother-in-law's soup tureen— (*Grace gasps. But can't keep from laughing*) Let's give it a try.

GRACE: What if somebody should find out?

GLORIA: No one's going to find out. Besides, this is an emergency. Here, let me prop you up with this. You'll tell me if I'm hurting you? (*Grace cringes in pain*) Like now!

GRACE (*settling down on the bowl*): Broke my hip last year. Had to go to the hospital. That's when they found the cancer. But my hip got better. Least 'til this mornin' when Roy brought me home in that pick-up truck 'o his.

Thought my bones was goin' to rattle right through my skin. (*A beat*) Listen, Honey, you don't have to stand there watching me. Been holdin' it so long it's goin' to take a while to get goin'.

GLORIA: I'll . . . unpack your suitcase.

GRACE: But I don't want you to—

GLORIA: No problem. That's all I've been doing since we arrived here. Unpacking.

GRACE: Seen pictures o' New York City on TV. All them people, the filth, the noise.

(*The bulldozers are still grumbling outside*)

GLORIA: You're trying to tell me it's quiet down here?

GRACE: Used to be. You say you live in town?

GLORIA: Uh-huh. We bought an old house there. We've been remodeling it all summer. (*Grace coughs, cringes in pain*) This prescription you left at the hospital. This is morphine, Mrs. Stiles. It's for pain.

GRACE: Oh, Honey, this ain't pain.

GLORIA: I've been through this with others. I know what kind—

GRACE: You ever been in labor?

GLORIA: Yes, I have.

GRACE: Then you know what pain really is.

GLORIA: I had them knock me out cold!

GRACE: Well I was wide awake. Up there in that "Big House?" I give birth to five baby boys. Five. And the smallest one weighed nine pounds. The first one, Roger Lee, he come out feet first, and I declare, he held on to my rib cage fourteen solid hours. Got through that without "morphine," I reckon— (*A loud roar from a bulldozer*) Oh. OH!

GLORIA (*alarmed*): What is it!

GRACE (*heavy sigh*): There it goes. Heaven be praised! Why, I'll bet Gabriella Stiles is turnin' somersaults in her grave.

GLORIA (*at the window*): Why are they digging so close to your house? (*Turning to the door*) I'm going to find out who's responsible for this.

GRACE: Now just hold on. They can dig where they want. They own it. All of it. I ought to know. I sold it to 'em. Even this cottage here. Goin' to knock this down soon as I die.

GLORIA: But why? What are they building out there?

GRACE: Some kind o' resort. "Time-shares" I think they call it. Gonna build a lake, ski slopes.

GLORIA: I read about this. Apple something?

GRACE: "Apple Glade."

GLORIA: That's it.

GRACE: Told 'em it was a foolish name. The orchard ain't even in a glade. 'S up there on that hill. There now, I think that just 'bout does it. Phew.

GLORIA: Would you like me to take that—

GRACE: No, just leave it for a while. You know, I'm sure you think you told me, but wou'ja mind tellin' me again. Who sent you here?

GLORIA: I did tell you. Okay. The organization I'm with, Hospice. We're a team of professionals who come into your home at this special time: a doctor, a nurse, a social worker. And volunteers, like me. We're all trained, meticulously trained. Then we're assigned cases. You'll be my third case.

GRACE: But just what is it you do?

GLORIA: We try to help people like you who are— Your doctor said he told you about your condition.

GRACE: You mean that I'm dying? Sure he told me. Said I got a few weeks. But no doctor's gonna tell me I'm dying.

GLORIA: Listen, it's perfectly normal to deny it at first. In fact, there's a whole series of steps—

GRACE: Deny it? Deny I'm goin' to die? Honey, when you're ninety years old, death don't come as no surprise.

Not only that, I buried my parents, my husband, and all five of my boys. All of 'em. If there's one thing I know about it's death. But tell me again, what on earth does my dyin' have to do with you?

GLORIA: I just want to help you, that's all.

GRACE: Help me what? Die?

GLORIA: In a way, yes.

GRACE: This is a new one on me. Perfect stranger shows up at my door and wants to help me die. Far as I know, it's the only thing in our whole lives we got to do by ourselves.

GLORIA: That's true, but now we've learned— Well, to manage it. I mean with the drugs we have today, there's no need for pain anymore or even discomfort. If you'd just let—

GRACE: You say you've done this before?

GLORIA: I've assisted on two other cases, yes.

GRACE: You helped two other perfect strangers die?

GLORIA: Yes.

GRACE: You do this for a living, help people die?

GLORIA: I told you, I'm a volunteer!

GRACE: You *volunteer* to help people die. Is this some sort o' Yankee custom I never heard about?

GLORIA: Why are you making this seem so ridiculous? You know you're a perfect example of what Hospice is all about! Your grandson, he picks you up from the hospital and dumps you here like a piece of refuse. You can't get anything to eat, anything to drink. You have no one to turn to for help. And believe me, Mrs. Stiles, you're going to need help! So even if it's only for a few hours a day, a woman in your condition shouldn't be left alone. (*The bulldozers pass by*) Especially with all that going on out there!

GRACE: But I'm not alone. The good Lord's here with me!

GLORIA: Oh, right. And just where was the good Lord all day when you needed help to go to the bathroom!

GRACE: He sent me someone to help, he sent me you! I just didn't recognize you at first.

GLORIA: Look, this hospice booklet. There are several stories in here about women just like you. Won't you at least read it?

GRACE: I don't think so.

GLORIA: Why?!

GRACE: In the first place I'm not interested! In the second—we'll just stop with the first place.

GLORIA: Mrs. Stiles, do you— You don't, do you? My god, that explains everything.

GRACE: I'm afraid I don't—

GLORIA: It's nothing to be ashamed of. Lots of people can't read. Why didn't you just tell the doctor? He thought you were—

GRACE: Ignorant? I didn't grow to be ninety years old by being ignorant!

GLORIA: I didn't say you were—

GRACE: I did learn to sign my name. That's all anyone cares about anyway. That I know how to sign my name! (*She moves, causing a slight spill*) Oh, now look what I've gone and done.

GLORIA (*hurrying to the bathroom*): Let me find a towel, then I'll get rid of that pot.

GRACE: Don't you have a family at home to take care of?

GLORIA: What?

GRACE: Or a job. Thought all you young women nowadays had jobs!

GLORIA (*hurrying back in with a couple of towels*): I had a job in New York. I've looked for something around here, but there isn't anything that even remotely— (*Blotting up the spill*) Anyway, the wife of my husband's partner suggested volunteering. Apparently, it's what all the well-off, married women here do with their spare time. It's more or less expected. That's when I heard about this new hospice program, that they were desperate for volunteers with professional skills. I am a college graduate, (*Looking down at the wet towel in her hands*) I have an MBA from Harvard. You see, my job at hospice is—well, I come in and help people settle things.

GRACE: But I don't have nothin' needs set'lin'. 'Cept plantin' me in the ground when the time comes, and I already made them arrangements.

GLORIA (*reaching under the covers for the tureen*): There's much more to hospice than what I do. Couldn't you just try it? For a week, a few days, Mrs. Stiles.

GRACE (*with Gloria's hands under her bottom*): Under the circumstances, honey, maybe you should call me Grace.

GLORIA (*withdrawing the pot and covering it with a towel*): Please, *Grace.*

GRACE: Just tell me one thing. What do you get out of this?

GLORIA: What? Nothing! Okay, let's just say I'm interested in—

GRACE: Death?

GLORIA: Yes.

GRACE: You can't even say the word.

GLORIA: Death.

GRACE: Well, I s'pose if you want to come up for a visit now and then I can't stop you.

GLORIA: I can't just visit! I told you, the work we do at Hospice, it's a "team" effort.

GRACE: Honey, there ain't enough room in here for a team! (*Looking at the tureen in Gloria's hands*) I really can't believe I did that in the family's good china. Talk about sinful.

GLORIA: Relax. Putting the wrong thing in the wrong china isn't sinful. Unless, of course, you're Kosher.

(*She's tickled by her own joke*)

GRACE: What's that mean?

GLORIA: Nothing. A little joke. Let me get rid of this and then I'll fix you that soup I brought. I hope you're hungry.

GRACE: I am, a little. But there's just one thing.

GLORIA: What's that?

GRACE: The soup tureen is slightly indisposed. (*Gloria looks down at the bowl*) That was a little joke of mine.

(*End of Scene One.*)

Scene 2

During the blackout we hear the roar of the earth movers as they tear away at the farm. The sound gradually fades into a country morning.

The lights reveal Grace propped up in bed. She's knitting. We hear the squawking of chickens outside, the crash of wood falling.

GLORIA (*off stage*): OW! DAMNIT!

GRACE: What's the matter?

GLORIA (*heavy sigh*): JUST A FINGERNAIL. (*Chickens squawk*) SHOO! GO AWAY! I SAID, SHOO! GRACE, THERE ARE CHICKENS ALL OVER THE PORCH!

GRACE: I usually feed 'em this time o' mornin'. (*Gloria enters with a load of cook stove wood. She's wearing an attractive dress under one of Grace's old aprons*) Still can't figure what you're doin' here so early. Ain't even eight o'clock.

GLORIA: I just dropped by to fix your breakfast.

GRACE: Oh sure, twenty miles up that mountain and you just stopped by.

GLORIA (*dumping the wood in a box near the stove*): What I mean is, I can't stay long. There's a reception later this morning for my husband. He's just been admitted to the Virginia bar and I'm expected to be there to help him celebrate. (*Dusting off her clothes*) Couldn't Roy have brought in some wood? Or does he charge you extra for that?

GRACE: You don't need to build a fire, I'm really not all that hungry.

GLORIA: I'm building a fire because it's freezing in here! (*Stuffing paper into the stove*) And you said you might eat an egg. I'm going to boil you an egg. Did you at least give Roy my list?

GRACE: Last night. He's none too happy 'bout havin' to drive into town this afternoon for a bed pan.

GLORIA: He should have had it here when you got home. Okay, the newspaper's in the stove.

GRACE: Now put in a few o' those kindlin' sticks. Three or four, that's all you need to start.

GLORIA (*looking at the stove*):   You sure you don't have something we can just—plug in?

GRACE: Don't like my breakfast cooked over 'lectricity. Tastes . . . bleh.

GLORIA (*stuffing in the wood*):   Good god, You're having a soft boiled egg. What difference does it make how you boil the water?

GRACE: Glorie, could I ask a favor? You seem to have acquired the unpleasant habit of usin' the Lord's name in vain.

GLORIA: What? When did I— You mean "good god?"

GRACE: It's just as easy to say "good heavens," or "good gravy."

GLORIA (*finding the matches*):   Good gravy. Yes, of course.

GRACE: Thank you. Now why don't you light the stove?

GLORIA: And my name is "Gloria."

GRACE: Oh yes.

GLORIA (*putting match to paper*):   You sure this thing is safe?

GRACE: That's right. Now close the door.

(*Gloria goes to the cottage door and closes it. Grace indicates the door on the stove*)

GLORIA: I knew that. (*She goes to the stove, closes the door*) Look at my hands. They are black. (*She turns to the hand pump*) How does this thing work?

GRACE: Got a handle. Got a spout. How do you think it works?

GLORIA (*taking off her wristwatch and pumping*):   Humor me, Grace. There's only so much "country" a person like me can absorb in one day.

(*The stove has started to smoke. Grace sees it. Gloria is pre-occupied with the pump*)

GRACE: Honey?

GLORIA: Why didn't your husband put a sink in the bathroom?

GRACE: We have a sink in the kitchen. Mr. Stiles didn't believe in excess. Honey, the stove.

GLORIA: When we remodeled our master bathroom I insisted on *two* sinks. Two sinks and a Jacuzzi!

GRACE: That's wonderful. About the stove—

GLORIA: What about the . . . (*She turns*)

GRACE: Now don't get excited.

GLORIA (*calmly, firmly in control*): I am not excited. I thought you said that thing was safe.

GRACE: It is, but I—

GLORIA (*starting for the phone*): And of course we don't have a phone to call for help.

(*The room is quickly filling with smoke*)

GRACE: We don't need—

GLORIA: And by the time I *pump* enough water *by hand*—

GRACE: We don't need water!

GLORIA: What are you trying to say, Grace? THE "GOOD LORD'S" GOING TO SHOW UP WITH A HOSE?!

GRACE: GO TURN THAT METAL THING STICKIN' OUT THE PIPE!

GLORIA: Why?

GRACE (*pushing her*): WILL YOU DO IT BEFORE WE CHOKE TO DEATH!

GLORIA: Okay, okay! (*As she turns the damper the stove makes a loud WHOOSH as the fire takes off*) HOLY JESUS! I'm sorry. I'm sorry! (*Fanning the smoke with her hands*) Grace, why don't I just drive into town and get you a nice sausage biscuit at Hardee's?

GRACE: Open the door. Smoke'll be gone in a minute.

GLORIA (*opening the door; chickens cackle*): Shoo! SHOO! Get out of here!

GRACE: Good heavens. Don't believe I've met anyone quite so . . .

GLORIA: Civilized!

GRACE: That's not the word I was lookin' for.

GLORIA: Look, I'm no girl scout, so sue me. (*Filling a pot with water*) Grace, I told you. We work together as a team. I don't have the training or the experience to do this by

27

myself. (*Turning with the pot in her hand*) Won't you please let me bring in the others?

GRACE: And just how many people's it goin' to take to heat that pan of water? (*Gloria turns, puts the pot on the stove*) Stove's hotter toward the back. (*Gloria moves the pan, setting it down a little firmer*)

GRACE: Put a top on that pan it'll boil faster. (*Gloria slams a top on the pot*) I'd put some more wood on the fire, that kindlin's probably 'bout gone.

GLORIA (*opening the firebox*): It's no wonder you country people eat a hearty breakfast. It's a day's work just to boil an egg! (*She stuffs a handful of sticks into the fire box. Shuts the door. Steps back*)

GRACE: Now don't stand there watchin' it.

GLORIA: Why?

GRACE: A watched pot never boils!

GLORIA: Since when?

GRACE (*her patience is wearing*): Just take my word for it! You'll find some fresh eggs there on the porch. Roy gathered them last night.

GLORIA: He gathered them? You mean like from . . . chickens.

GRACE: That's where eggs come from. From chickens.

GLORIA (*stepping outside, the chickens flutter*):   Go away! SHOO!

GRACE: If you'd throw a handful of that feed out in the yard they wouldn't bother you!

GLORIA: You want me to feed them?

GRACE: I don't *want* you to do nothin'!

GLORIA (*entering with a bucket of eggs*):   Oh, yuck. Grace these eggs have bird shi— "doo" all over them!

GRACE: THEN WASH THEM OFF! Know somethin', honey. I think it would be a whole lot easier if you got into bed and I got up and made breakfast for you!

GLORIA: How many eggs would you like?

GRACE: I would like one. But you have as many as you want.

GLORIA (*holding up a dirty egg*):   I don't care for any, thanks.

GRACE: All this for one egg.

GLORIA: Tell me about it. How about a nice slice of toa— (*She looks at the stove*) On second thought . . .

GRACE: There happens to be a toaster right there in front of you.

29

GLORIA (*lifting the toaster cover*): A toaster? It is a toaster! And it's electric!

GRACE: Contrary to what you might think, the twentieth century has found its way out to this farm.

GLORIA: Okay, I can do this now. There's just one thing. How am I supposed to tell when the water is boiling?

GRACE: You lift the lid off the pot and look.

GLORIA: But you told me not to.

GRACE: I told you not to watch it, I didn't tell you not to— (*Gloria smiles*) You're teasing me! You know all my life I regretted the fact I never had a daughter. Now I'm wondering if I wasn't blessed! (*The telephone rings*) What on earth? (*Gloria looks at Grace. Smiles*) They told me it would take two weeks.

GLORIA (*answering the phone*): Stiles' residence, Gloria Whitmore speaking. . . . Ah, Mr. Huntley . . . Yes, it's working fine . . . You should be sorry . . . One moment, I'll ask her. (*To Grace*) This is the district manager of the telephone company? He's so sorry for the interruption of your service, he wonders if you'll accept six free months of call-waiting.

GRACE: Six months o' what?

GLORIA (*into the phone*): She'd love it . . . Don't worry, Mr. Huntley, I will. (*She hangs up*)

GRACE: Just what kind of job did you have there in New York City?

GLORIA: I was with a national consulting firm. We—how shall I put it—we "fixed" businesses. You know, large corporations that were in trouble. In fact—

(*A loud chain saw starts up outside*)

GRACE: Must be eight o'clock.

GLORIA (*crossing to the door*): GRACE, I'M GOING TO STOP THIS!

GRACE: NOW YOU JUST HOLD ON.

GLORIA: I WON'T HAVE YOU SPENDING THE LAST DAYS OF YOUR LIFE—

GRACE: THIS IS MY BUSINESS AND I WON'T HAVE YOU MESSIN' WITH IT! NOW CLOSE THAT DOOR!

GLORIA (*closing the door*): When you sold the farm, didn't you . . . There's a standard paragraph lawyers use entitling you to *quiet* possession and *peaceful* enjoyment!

GRACE: Didn't have no lawyer.

GLORIA: You sold a five hundred acre farm and you didn't have—

GRACE: Fellow at the bank took care of everything. I didn't want to sell, but with Roger Lee gone—

GLORIA: Roger Lee?

GRACE: Roy's father. He'd been runnin' the farm ever since Mr. Stiles passed away. But then he got the cancer—

GLORIA: What about Roy, didn't he—

GRACE: Roy ain't no farmer. All he cares 'bout are cars. Then I broke my hip. Hospital bills alone was 'nough to choke a mule. Then this big developer from Northern Virginia come along. Said he'd give me a fair price for the farm, let me live down here in the cottage 'til I died.

GLORIA: How generous of him.

GRACE: And he said he'd name his resort after my orchard. Fellow at the bank said I might not get another offer like this. If I didn't take it and the bank had to foreclose, I might lose everything, end up in some county nursin' home. (*The crash of a huge tree falling*) Listen, they're cuttin' down the trees up at the big house. It's so sad. Why them oak trees been standin' there since George Washington was a boy.

GLORIA: Why won't you let me go out there and make them stop?

GRACE: There's nothin' you can do. Go check that water, it's probably close to boilin'. (*Gloria burns her fingers on the pot lid, tries to stifle a "goddamnit"*) There's pot-holders right in front of you.

GLORIA: Thanks. (*Surprised*) It *is* boiling.

GRACE: One of the Lord's little miracles.

GLORIA: Three minutes, right?

GRACE: Make it four.

GLORIA: Let me get my watch.

GRACE: That's all right, I'll count.

GLORIA: You'll what?

GRACE: With my knittin'. Arthritis and all, I still knit about sixty stitches a minute. I'll let you know when I've knitted two hundred and forty. Go ahead, drop in the egg.

GLORIA: You're serious. Okay. (*Dropping in the egg*) There. (*Gloria picks her watch up from the sink, sneaks a peek, stands there, arms folded*)

GRACE: Oh, we don't have to stop talking. I can knit and count and talk at the same time.

GLORIA: You're putting me on.

GRACE: Nine, ten, eleven, twelve. It's really very simple.

GLORIA: What's that you're knitting?

GRACE: A sweater. I have a great niece lives in Mobile. Name's Luanne. Let's see, she's my youngest older brother's middle son's first daughter's third child. By her second marriage. Anyway, Luanne writes to me. Only person in the whole world writes to me. And I know what you're thinkin'. Roy reads her letters to me. Always wished I could write her back. Tell her 'bout me. She's fascinated 'cause I'm her oldest living relative.

GLORIA: How old is she?

GRACE: She'll be thirteen in July. Last summer after Roger Lee died? Luanne's mamma called me, said Luanne wanted to come up and visit me. All the way from Mobile. I was livin' up at the Big House then. A few days before they was due, I was hurryin' about tryin' to pick up the place. That's when I slipped and fell. Roy had to call 'em, tell 'em not to come. I thought I'd put this sweater in a box. Ask Roy to mail it come July. Think he'll remember? Men are so careless 'bout such things.

GLORIA: I'll mail it for you.

GRACE: Oh no, I couldn't ask—

GLORIA (*taking out her notebook and writing*): Consider it done.

GRACE: You sure? I shouldn't say this, but I would feel better leavin' it with you.

GLORIA: I'll need Luanne's address, of course.

GRACE: I'll have Roy get it for you. And money for the postage.

GLORIA: How are we doing on our egg?

GRACE: Hundred thirty-two, hundred thirty-three.

GLORIA: I tried to knit once. And crochet, embroider. My parents always gave me gifts that were . . . "gender specific." Like little stitchery kits. I would dutifully start each and every project. They would last a few days . . .

GRACE: You young people don't have time for this sort of thing no more. When I was a girl we had nothin' to do, 'specially winter nights, 'cept sit around near the fire. And since we lived by the rule, "idle hands are the devil's workshop," someone always made sure our hands were never idle.

GLORIA: When we were moving here I came across a box filled with all those half-finished kits. I don't know why, but I hang on to all kinds of junk like that.

GRACE: It's a woman's way. We're savers. I believe the time is . . . up.

GLORIA: What?

GRACE: The egg.

GLORIA: The egg! Look at that. Four minutes on the nose. You're an amazing woman, Grace.

GRACE: "Amazin' Grace." That was always my favorite hymn back when I went to church. You mentioned your parents. They still livin'?

GLORIA (*preparing the egg*):   Oh, yes. They live down in Palm Beach. Dad's retired. Which means he sits home all day and drives my mother crazy. Which means she calls me two or three times a week to drive me crazy. How do you like your toast?

GRACE: Just shy o' burnt. Your mother, is she happy?

GLORIA (*crossing to the fridge for the butter*):   She thinks she is.

GRACE: She *thinks* she's happy. That different from, you know, just being happy?

GLORIA: It's a question of expectations, Grace. My mother's never had any. At least none that weren't furnished by my father. I mean Daddy's idea of the female sex is blatantly Neanderthal. When I was in high school I'd bring home report cards that were, I kid you not, solid columns of "A" pluses. Know what he'd say? "What a shame to waste such brains on a girl." Oo, I wanted to— Anyway, I was sent off to college to major, appropriately, in the arts. Poor Daddy. He almost had a coronary when he found out I had switched my major to business.

GRACE: And you were an only child?

GLORIA: Yes.

GRACE: And how old are your children?

GLORIA: Pardon me?

GRACE: You said yesterday you went through labor. I just figured—

GLORIA: We had a son. Danny. He was killed in an automobile accident a couple of years ago.

GRACE: You poor thing.

GLORIA: That's okay. I've had plenty of time to learn to deal with it.

GRACE: These young people today and their automobiles. Why do they insist on driving so fast?

GLORIA: Danny was only twelve years old. He wasn't driving, I was. Would you like salt on your egg?

GRACE (*after a moment*): Yes. Lots of salt. And lots of butter on the toast.

GLORIA (*salting the egg*): Too much salt and butter, Grace. They say it'll take ten years off your . . . (*Realizing what she's saying, she shakes on more salt*)

GRACE: Ter'ble thing to lose a child. My Carroll died when he was a baby. Went in to check on him one morning and he wasn't breathin'. Doctor come. Said these things just happen. Few years later Duane was out huntin' with his Daddy. Tripped over some barbed wire buried under the snow? Gun went off. He was ten years old. Got so I hated to let the little ones out o' my sight. Thought I was goin' to lose 'em all. Guess I did, though, didn't I? Collin in the war. Ronnie in a minin' accident near Cumberland. Only one to really grow up was Roger Lee. Always said, Roger Lee was born hangin' on and he hung on to life longer'n all the rest of 'em. Guess my only comfort is I'll be seein' em all real soon now.

GLORIA (*carrying a tray to the bed*):   Here we are. One stiff, soft boiled egg, and one piece of black toast drenched in butter.

GRACE: Looks pretty as a picture.

GLORIA: Do you really believe that? About seein' your children in another life?

GRACE: Course I do, don't you?

GLORIA: I . . . No.

GRACE: S'pose next you're goin' to say you don't believe in God. You and Bernice Wallace. Why is the good Lord sendin' so many heathens 'cross my path?

GLORIA: Come on, Grace, eat your egg.

GRACE: Try as I might, I . . . I'm just not hungry.

GLORIA: Not hungry! After I risked life and limb on that stove? Come on. You have to keep up your strength. (*A beat*) Okay, okay.

GRACE: I'll probably have an appetite later. Just put it on that shelf above the stove. It'll keep warm there.

GLORIA: Speaking of which, it is more comfortable in here. I think I'll heat some water for the dishes.

GRACE: The water's already hot.

GLORIA: You have a water heater? I didn't—

GRACE: There in the stove. Lift that lid on the right side. Use a pot-holder! You see? A wood stove not only cooks the food and warms the room. It also heats the water for the dishes. Without usin' one speck o' 'lectricity or one drop o' that A-rab oil.

GLORIA: I'll wash up these few things.

GRACE: Just leave 'em. You said you had a reception to go to.

GLORIA (*carrying an enameled dish pan to the stove*): I have a few minutes.

GRACE: And you're probably used to one of them dishwashin' machines.

GLORIA: Yes, but I think I can figure out how to wash a pot.

GRACE: Careful now. That water gets mighty hot.

GLORIA: I know it does.

GRACE: Use that ladle there.

GLORIA: Grace, I can do this, okay?

GRACE: 'Course you can. You are a college educated woman. (*Ladling the water into the pan*) 'Cept that pan's metal, honey! I wouldn't try holdin' it while you was—

(*Gloria screams and runs to the sink*)

GLORIA: SHIT! Shit-shit-shit-shit-shit-shit-shit-shit SHIT! (*She throws the pan into the sink. Stands there fanning the air with her burned hand*) I'm sorry, Grace, but there are times when "good gravy" JUST DOESN'T CUT IT!

GRACE: Honey, would you please just leave!

(*We hear a deafening siren blast*)

GLORIA: That does it! (*She opens the door. The chickens cackle*) Shoo! Get out of my way. I SAID GET! (*There's a piercing rooster crow, a huge fluttering flare-up, Gloria screams, runs back inside and slams the door*) THAT THING ATTACKED ME! ON IT'S WORST DAY, NEW YORK WAS NEVER LIKE THIS!

GRACE: Honey, I mean it. It was thoughtful of you to come here today but now I want you to get your things and go home!

GLORIA: I've upset you. I'm sorry. I'm all right now. Just let me clean up these few things.

GRACE: You really don't—

GLORIA: Where do you keep the soap?

GRACE: Under the sink.

(*Gloria reaches under the sink. She yanks her hand back and screams*)

GRACE: Honey! Honey, what is it? (*Gloria runs to the chair, sits*) Did you hurt yourself? Did—

GLORIA: A RAT! Ran right across my hand! Oh, god, I think I'm going to be sick.

GRACE: Couldn't have been a rat. A large mouse, yes, but not a rat.

GLORIA: What difference does it make!

GRACE: It's that time of year. Mice're movin' in for the winter. (*Gloria pulls her legs up*) Relax, we'll set a few traps. (*Gloria sits trembling, holding up her burned left hand, her defiled right hand*) Honey? Honey, you okay?

GLORIA: Yes. I'm sorry. (*She does some kind of relaxing exercise, her finger on her pulse*) I really am sorry. If you'll just give me a few moments . . .

GRACE: Now you just take your time. (*A beat*) I can wait.

GLORIA: You need something. What is it? Just tell me and I'll—

GRACE: No. I mean—well all this excitement, I do believe I have to go to the bathroom. But I can hold it!

GLORIA: Don't be silly, I'll get Gabriella's—

GRACE: No, I mean *to* the bathroom. I think I could do it today.

GLORIA: You're sure?

GRACE: I'm so tired of lying in this bed.

GLORIA (*helping Grace to her feet*):   All right. But you'll stop if there's any pain.

GRACE: I'm really sorry about that mouse.

GLORIA: It was a rat.

GRACE: 'Course it was. Oh, it feels so good to be standin' up.

GLORIA: Your hip doesn't hurt?

(*They start toward the bathroom*)

GRACE (*shaking her head*):   You know what's funny? My hip has mended itself beautiful. Now tell me somethin', why would one piece of me be gettin' better while at the same time the rest of me is dyin'?

(*There is a terrific explosion. The room shakes. Dust falls from the ceiling, dishes fall from the kitchen shelves*)

GLORIA: WHAT WAS THAT!

GRACE (*matter of fact*):   Sounded like dynamite.

GLORIA: Dynamite? Dynamite. (*Breaking down*) Oh, Grace. (*Breathing rapidly*) I don't know. I just— Oh no, I think I'm hyperventilating!

GRACE (*holding up Gloria as they continue walking*): Glorie, honey, don't worry. Grace is here. I'll take care of you. I'll take care of you.

(*The lights fade out*)

(*End of Scene 2.*)

Scene 3

During the blackout we continue to hear sirens and explosions as the mountain is blasted away. Finally, it's night, the following Friday. We hear tree frogs and crickets. Grace is sitting in the rocker. She's in great pain. She wears an old robe over her nightgown. From the bathroom we hear someone rinsing things out in the tub. Grace sits back. Her breathing slows a little. Gloria enters wearing a pair of slacks, a blouse with the sleeves rolled up. Her hair is a mess. She's exhausted.

GLORIA: I've rinsed everything out. I don't think the stains will set.

GRACE: Corn starch. You put corn starch on blood stains.

GLORIA: You told me. I did that. How are you feeling? (*Grace shakes her head*) Grace, please. Take the morphine.

GRACE: No!

GLORIA: It will ease the pain!

GRACE: It will put me to sleep!

GLORIA: Good! I haven't seen you close your eyes in five days!

GRACE: I said no!

GLORIA: I can't stand seeing you suffer like this!

GRACE (*snapping at her*):   Who is the morphine for, me or you?

GLORIA: I'm calling your doctor!

GRACE: Put that thing down!

GLORIA: You were throwing up blood!

GRACE: Honey, you didn't come here to help me pull through this. You came here to help me die!

GLORIA (*putting down the phone*):   You shouldn't have been up so much today.

GRACE: It was wonderful to be up. First day all week them fool machines outside been quiet. I'd still like to know how you got 'em to stop.

GLORIA: It was easy, I sent Peter to find a judge who would agree that a sick, old woman shouldn't be subjected to bulldozers, chain saws, and dynamite!

GRACE: You trying to say you did it for me?

GLORIA: Yes I did it for you!

GRACE: Even so, it was nice to be able to hear the birds today.

GLORIA: Don't get used to it. The judge thinks you should go back to the hospital.

GRACE: Does he now? And is the judge goin' to pay for it?

GLORIA: The government will pay for it, Grace.

GRACE: But I don't want to be in the hospital! This is where I want to die. Not some cold, Pine-sol smellin' room!

GLORIA: Relax. Peter's trying to set up a meeting with the developer tomorrow and . . . Come to think of it, he was supposed to call me.

GRACE: He's wonderin' where you are. All week you've been goin' home in the middle of the afternoon. Please go on. Roy'll be along any minute.

GLORIA: At midnight? Roy hasn't been staying with you, has he? (*Grace doesn't answer*) You told me he stayed with you every night.

GRACE: He does. 'Til I go to sleep.

GLORIA: And just when do you go to sleep?

GRACE: I let Roy stay till 'bout eight. Then I close my eyes and pretend to sleep.

GLORIA: Why?

GRACE: So he'll go home! Roy has better things to do than to babysit a half dead old woman. Just like you got better things to do. (*Gloria sits down*) Well, if we're goin' to just sit here burnin' the 'lectricity you might as well fetch me my knittin'. I believe it's—

GLORIA: I have it. Here.

GRACE: Thank you. Look. I just finished the sleeves. All I got left is a little bit of the neck.

GLORIA: Oh, Grace. That's beautiful. It looks like—

GRACE: It is. The apple orchard on the hill. Thought it would be nice if Luanne could see what it looked like. You know that orchard's the only part of this farm that was all mine. Started every one of them trees myself. From seeds I gathered from other farms 'round here.

GLORIA: May I hold it?

GRACE: Course the trees are old and gnarly now, but they still bear the finest apples you ever tasted. I really don't think I could have survived here long as I have if it wasn't for that orchard. It's where I used to go to get away from Mr. Stiles, his mamma, my kids. It was where I could . . . let my mind go, let it wander far away as it pleased.

GLORIA: This is a work of art.

GRACE: Mmm.

GLORIA: And look, you're knitting the front and back at the same time.

GRACE: My grandma taught me that when I was just a girl. She called it "the old way." See you don't knit the sweater in pieces like they do today. You knit it all at once, even the sleeves. That way you don't have no seams.

GLORIA: I wish I had the patience for things like this.

GRACE: You could learn.

GLORIA: Maybe tomorrow. (*Handing the sweater back to Grace*) Thank you.

(*Grace knits. Gloria sits on the bed picking at her fingernails. Grace becomes more and more irritated with the sound and the fact that Gloria is just sitting there in idleness. Finally, when she can't take it any more . . .*)

GRACE: Would you like me to find something for you to do!

GLORIA (*a little startled*): What?

GRACE: I asked if you would like—

GLORIA: Oh, no. I'm fine.

GRACE: But you're just sittin' there.

GLORIA: I'm thinking.

GRACE: But you're not doin' nothing.

GLORIA: I'm thinking.

GRACE: Thinkin' is not doin'. Thinkin' is just a fancy word for idleness. And—

GRACE/GLORIA: "Idleness is the devil's workshop."

GRACE: It is, indeed. And I will not be party to contributin' one speck of anything to the devil.

GLORIA: I don't believe in the devil, Grace.

GRACE: You think the devil cares? And that sound. Picking, picking. Why are you doing that to your hands?

GLORIA: Because in the last five days, look. I have broken every one of my fingernails. Every one!

GRACE: Then go home. Sit in your fancy Jacuzzi. Let your fingernails grow back!

GLORIA (*jumping up, going into the dark kitchen*):   I'll find something to do!

GRACE: Thank you. (*A beat*) There's a bag of fabric scraps under this table.

GLORIA: I don't sew.

GRACE: This ain't sewin' it's cuttin'. Just come get the bag and I'll show you.

(*Gloria goes after the fabric while Grace digs a pair of scissors and a square of cardboard from her knitting bag*)

GRACE: You ask me, Glorie, your biggest problem is you think too much. Nothin' in this whole world ever got done by sittin' 'round thinkin' about it. And that's a fact.

GLORIA: Yes, Grace.

GRACE: And don't talk to me in that tone. I'm not your mother. (*Gloria returns with the bag*) All right, now here. Just put this piece of cardboard top of the cloth and cut around it. Think you can do that?

(*Gloria sits on the bed, cuts the fabric*)

GLORIA: What's this for?

GRACE: For a quilt top I'm plannin' to make. And don't tell me I won't live long enough to finish it. Makes no difference. I take great comfort knowing no matter how long I live I'll have plenty to do.

GLORIA (*holding up the first piece*): How's that?

GRACE: A work o' art. Do another.

GLORIA (*cutting the fabric*): Why do you keep calling me "Glorie"?

GRACE: I'm still doin' that? (*Gloria smiles and nods. Grace laughs*) When I was just a girl, there was this hymn my Mama liked to sing. Called "Where He Leads Me." The last part, it goes (*Singing*) "He will give me grace and glory, and go with me all the way." Mama used to laugh. "We got our little Grace," she'd say. "Now all we need is a little Glorie." 'Course she never got her little Glorie. Neither did I. (*Noticing Gloria has stopped cutting*) I didn't mean to set you off thinkin' again, go on, keep cuttin' out them squares!

GLORIA: You're too much, Grace.

GRACE: I'm amazin'. You said so yourself. You remind me of my husband. Mr. Stiles. He was always thinkin', too. Dark, broodin' thoughts. They was all like that. All them Stiles. Had this streak o' gloom in 'em. All they ever saw was the dark side o' life. Not that it's ever been easy here-abouts, but like I just said, in my family we laughed, we sang. We were always happy just to be alive. But with them Stiles, whenever you ran into one, it was like a cloud passed front of the sun.

GLORIA: Why did you marry him? "Mr." Stiles.

GRACE: Oh, he wasn't bad lookin'. He was a hard worker. So he had a gloomy streak.

GLORIA: Roy's like that, too, isn't he?

GRACE: He is indeed. My good blood's been swallowed up by the blood of them gloomy Stiles.

GLORIA: He's been avoiding me all week. Whenever he sees me coming he goes the other way.

GRACE: Roy's suspicious. Thinks you're up here after something.

GLORIA: Like what?

GRACE: My money, I guess.

GLORIA: I thought you didn't have any money.

GRACE: I don't. But that ain't enough to keep Roy from being suspicious.

GLORIA: Even if you had money, I certainly don't need it.

GRACE: That's what I told Roy. Told him you were just a wealthy young woman with more time on her hands than sense.

GLORIA: Thanks a lot.

GRACE: Roy always thought he'd have an inheritance from me. He would've, too, if his Daddy and me could've just died like normal people 'stead of messin' with them doctors. They told Roger Lee if they didn't operate he'd be dead in six months. So they operated. He was dead in a week. And look at me. Oh, sure, them doctors, they slowed it down some. So now instead of dyin' I just sit shrivelin' up like a . . . piece o' old fruit. (*Gloria yawns, stretches*) Look at you. Why don't you go home?

GLORIA: I'm not leaving you here alone. Not after what you've just been through.

GRACE: Told you, I don't need a baby sitter.

GLORIA: Are you going to let me put you to bed?

GRACE: No!

GLORIA: Grace, please! I'm beat. And I'm scared!

GRACE: Thought you said you done this before. Helped people die.

GLORIA: They were two, sweet old men. Quiet, cooperative, AND HAPPY TO TAKE THEIR DRUGS!

GRACE: Were they now?

GLORIA: I need sleep!

GRACE: Who's stoppin' you? Go ahead, lie down.

GLORIA: I am not going to sleep in your bed!

GRACE: I'm not using it.

GLORIA: You intend to sit there all night?

GRACE: Yes!

GLORIA: Why?

GRACE: Because! (*Gloria, screams, throws herself on the bed*) Because . . . I don't want to be asleep when He comes.

GLORIA: When who comes?

GRACE: Death. Oh, I'm afraid of Him, I am. But it's the kind o' fear—I don't quite know how to—It's like this time my Daddy hauled us kids all the way to Richmond to the State Fair. They had this ferris wheel there. Looked to be least a mile high. I wanted to ride that thing mor'n anything in the world, but I was too scared. My whole life's been like that. Always too scared. Now Death's coming to call. And I'm frightened. But this time I'm ready—Oh, mercy, I am ready! To be lifted up into that Promised

Place (*Breaking down*) where I won't hurt or be afraid ever again.

(*Gloria goes to her but Grace, embarrassed pushes her away. Gloria goes to the phone*)

GLORIA: Let me call Peter to tell him not to wait up.

GRACE: I really don't need your wore-out company. Why don't you go home and take care of somebody does need you? Like that poor husband o' yours.

GLORIA: Peter's a big boy. He can take care of himself. Listen to that. Our machine. Twelve o'clock and the creep's not even home. (*Into the phone*) Yes, it's me. What's going on? You were supposed to call me. I guess I'll have to assume you finished everything on the list I gave you. Like setting up a meeting with that developer? Peter, you know how important this is to me. If you don't want to help don't jerk me around, just say so. Listen, I have to stay here tonight.

GRACE: Who says you have to stay here?

GLORIA: I'll see you first thing in the morning. (*She hangs up*)

GRACE: I don't like this. The way you talked to that man. And where is he so late? Bet he's out lookin' for you.

GLORIA (*sitting on the bed, exhausted*): Don't be silly. It's Friday night. He's out drinking with the boys. Ever since we moved here Peter's been heavily into male bonding.

GRACE: Into what?

GLORIA (*yawning*): It's a guy thing. It's like—spitting.
(*Lying back*)

GRACE (*going to the bed*): Let's pull this quilt up 'fore you
catch a chill.

GLORIA: I'm fine, Grace. Stop fussing over me.

GRACE: I want to fuss I'll fuss! Just told you I regretted
not havin' a daughter. That was true. Always felt I had so
much to give, so many secrets to share. Boy children, they
ain't interested in learnin' nothin'. All they want to do is
break away. Get out and tear up the earth. You know I've
always marveled the human race has been able to survive
long as it has in the hands of men.

GLORIA: You sound like a liberated woman, Grace. I'm
impressed.

GRACE: Sure, I'm liberated all right. Ain't been mor'n
fifty miles from this farm since the day I got married.
Honey, you can close your eyes. Don't worry, if I see
death comin' I'll wake you.

GLORIA: Okay, okay.

(*She settles back. It's quiet for a moment*)

GRACE: What I just said, 'bout boy children tearing up
the earth? I wasn't talkin' 'bout your little boy.

GLORIA: I know.

GRACE: He wasn't like that, was he?

GLORIA: No.

GRACE: What was his name? Danny?

GLORIA: Yes.

GRACE: Bet he was smart.

GLORIA: Yes. (*A beat*) But he was still very much a boy. My husband saw to that. But for every jock thing Peter pushed Danny into, I insisted on equal time. Like with his piano. Not that he was a child prodigy, but he did have talent. I mean he was only twelve years old, and already developing his own style— as his teacher would say, (*Imitating the teacher*) "somewhere between Vladimir Horowitz and Stevie Wonder." But what was most unusual about Danny was the incredibly high standards he'd set for himself. He reminded me of— me when I was his age.

GRACE: Just look at your face. All lit up. Wondered if I'd ever see you smile like that.

GLORIA: Oh, Grace, that was such a time in my life. I had just moved to a very large firm, brought in, I might add, as full partner. Know what that means? It means I had made it to the top. I finally had power, Grace. And money. I mean real money. I could now afford to send Danny to an extraordinary new school. We found this huge old apartment right on the East River. With its own garage. I bought a car. An expensive car. But even more than the money or the power, I had finally achieved, as a woman, respect. Even my father was mutely impressed. Oh, and I began having an affair. (*Gloria is startled by a loud snap! The tiny cry of a mouse caught in a trap*) There goes another . . . "large" mouse.

GRACE: Look at you. You never even screamed that time.

GLORIA: I just hate it when they cry like that.

GRACE: They don't suffer much. And they're blessed with not havin' the wits to know they're dyin'.

GLORIA: I suppose. Your children. The ones you lost when they were small. Duane and . . .

GRACE: Carroll.

GLORIA: How did you deal with . . . losing them?

GRACE: Deal with it? I'm not sure I know what you mean. I grieved. Still do. But it was the good Lord's will.

GLORIA: And you didn't question it? The good Lord's will?

GRACE: What I don't think a person like you understands, people like us, people tied to the earth, we're used to death. It's never pretty, at times it's mighty inconvenient, but it's happenin' 'round us every minute just the same. Look outside, it's the middle o' fall. What do you think's goin' on out there? You civilized people. You've moved so far away from death you forget it's as much a part of life as being born. Like the doctor said, these things just happen.

GLORIA (*rising, going to the kitchen area*):   Oh yes, it certainly did happen. One warm, September afternoon . . .

GRACE: Honey, don't—

GLORIA: . . . it had been Danny's first day at the *new* school. I decided to pick him up. In the *new* car. We were heading back across town. I don't know where it came from. The newspaper truck. When it hit us, it crumpled Danny's side of our car like a paper bag. We were pinned inside the wreck for more than an hour. The collision had squeezed us into this tight sliver of space. Danny was on my lap. And as I held him I could feel his life slowly slipping from his body. And there was nothing I could do. But scream.

So we buried him. This gentle, gifted boy. Disposed of his clothes, his—things. And then, I don't know, I just shut down. Wouldn't go to work. Wouldn't answer the phone. Wouldn't even go outside. There didn't seem to be any point. Peter dragged me from one doctor to another. We ended up with a shrink who suggested a change, somewhere far from the city. Peter was thrilled. He'd always hated New York—the pace, the competition. He began calling his old law school buddies until he found— Don't ask me why I came with him. I guess, at the time, I could have cared less where I lived. So now here I am, stuck in this—

GRACE: Why don't you lie back—

GLORIA: What still gnaws at me. Okay, maybe I did deserve to get slapped down. I mean, I had become a little lofty, a little full of myself. Peter was feeling very threatened by my success and I was loving it. And there was the

Lucy Arnaz (*left*) as Glorie and Estelle Parsons as Grace.

All photographs of the 1996 Off Broadway Production at the Laura Pels Theatre at the Roundabout, in New York City, by Carol Rosegg.

Lucy Arnaz as Glorie and Estelle Parsons as Grace.

Lucy Arnaz as Glorie and Estelle Parsons as Grace.

Lucy Arnaz as Glorie and Estelle Parsons as Grace.

affair. But if these were my sins, *MY* SINS, why was it Danny who paid for them? That's what's insane. That's what makes me want to— You talk about God? What kind of God is this? Is he sick? Is he a sadist? If he's not butchering us outright he's . . . Look at your life. Haven't you ever asked yourself . . . (*She stops. Gropes for control*) I'm sorry. I . . . I don't know why I'm doing this.

GRACE: My life. What about my life?

GLORIA: No.

GRACE: Say it.

GLORIA (*trying to push it back but can't*): You buried not one child, but five! Everything you've ever worked for has been reduced to— Look out there. To rubble! You have a grandson. Who are you to him? A woman he charges to run errands and cut wood. Haven't you ever asked yourself what your life's been for? Here you are a sick old woman, ravaged with pain, without a soul in the world to even care whether you live or—Grace, I— (*Going after her coat and purse*) I think I'd better go home after all.

GRACE: I never have asked myself that question. What's my life been for.

GLORIA: Grace—

GRACE: Maybe I should.

GLORIA: I didn't mean—

GRACE: I sure ain't left my mark on much o' nothin'.

GLORIA: Don't say that. You've had a wonderful life.

GRACE: Ha!

GLORIA: You didn't live to be ninety years old by—

GRACE: I've lived to be ninety years old by stayin' busy! That's how I done it. Stayed busy!

GLORIA: Grace, I'm sorry.

GRACE: Why should you be sorry for my miserable life? Got nothin' to do with you. I'd still like to know what you're doin' here, messin' with death. So you lost a child. Like the doctor said—

GLORIA: Things happen.

GRACE: Yes.

GLORIA: Just happen. No rhyme, no reason. No one pulling the strings.

GRACE: I didn't say there was no reason.

GLORIA: Then what is it?

GRACE: How should I know? You accept each day as it comes. You don't question.

GLORIA: No questions.

GRACE: No.

GLORIA: Just stay busy. That's what I'm supposed to do? Stay busy for the next fifty years?

GRACE: Told you I don't know! Something like this happens you start over.

GLORIA: Of course. That's my husband's answer. Maybe even have another baby. So that in a few years— Look how many children you buried. And you're telling me I can go through this hell again?

GRACE: I ain't tellin' you nothin'! Good heavens, honey, either you do a thing or you don't. What other choice you got?

GLORIA: Oh, I've got choices. At least a few.

GRACE: Like what? Oh. Oh, I see. (*Slowly standing*) That what this is, this volunteerin' you do? You here to try Death on for size 'fore you go off and kill yourself? Is that it? IS IT!

GLORIA: THIS SHOULDN'T HAVE HAPPENED, GODDAMNIT! He was a brilliant, innocent boy with his whole life in front of him, not some miserable rodent stumbling into a trap! You're the one with the faith, you tell me! What heavenly purpose was served by crushing his beautiful, young body and leaving it on my lap to die? All I want is an answer, Grace! One lousy reason! (*A beat*) Except there is no answer, is there? I'm sorry, but whatever this—game is, I can't play it anymore! (*She hurries toward the front door*)

GRACE: Glorie, honey, would you do me a favor? (*Gloria stops*) Would you let me go first?

(*Gloria looks at Grace for a moment. Then hurries out as the lights go to black*)

END OF ACT I

ACT
TWO

ACT II

Scene 1

A gospel quartet is singing a spirited version of the traditional hymn, "Close to Thee." It's late the next morning. Neither Grace nor Gloria are seen. There is a sound on the front porch.

GLORIA: Grace! It's me! (*Gloria, wearing a coat, pushes the door open and enters carrying a grocery bag, a large black canvas bag, her attache case*) Grace? Sorry I'm so late. (*She dumps her things on the chest of drawers and takes off her coat*) I was in meetings all morning, then the supermarket was crowded. . . . (*Realizing she can't see Grace*) Grace? (*She looks on the other side of the bed*) Grace? (*She hurries into the bathroom*) GRACE! (*The back door opens and Grace enters wearing an old coat. She has the Walkman headset over her ears and is carrying an apron full of apples. Gloria comes out of the bathroom*) GOOD GRAVY, GRACE, YOU SCARED THE PISS OUT OF ME!

GRACE: How's that?

GLORIA: I said . . . (*Removing the headset*) What are you doing up?

GRACE: Went up to visit my orchard. Found these apples on the ground, thought I'd make a pie.

GLORIA: Let me help you with . . .

GRACE: Get a pan! (*Gloria hurries into the kitchen*) Did you see it out there? The farm?

GLORIA: Yes, I've seen it.

GRACE: What it took Mr. Stiles and me our whole lives to build. Gone. Scraped away.

GLORIA (*holding the pan as Grace unloads the apples*): Grace, this is heavy.

GRACE: Why you wouldn't know our family ever lived here at all. (*Hanging up her coat*) Wasn't sure I'd ever see you back here. Fact, the way you left here last night— talkin' 'bout takin' your own life—

GLORIA: Grace, I was exhausted. I said things—

GRACE: You said you was thinkin' o' killin' yourself.

GLORIA: I know what I said.

GRACE: Is it true?

GLORIA: It was a mistake. And I'm sorry. Please Grace. I came back this morning to see if we could begin again. Start fresh. For example, I'm here with a clear conscience. I called Winnie Burns this morning. She's the dear woman who runs the hospice program, and I resigned.

GRACE: You didn't have to do that for me.

GLORIA: It wasn't for you. It was for me. (*Unloading the bags*) But now this. This *is* for you. I mean for both of us. I hope you're hungry, because I'm famished.

GRACE: Thought maybe I'd have an apple.

GLORIA: We'll save the apples for dessert. Now before I show you what I bought, let me say I know everything might seem a little strange at first. But once you taste it. Oh, Grace, I know I went crazy, but they just opened a new deli in the supermarket. Everything's imported. From New York. Now you just sit there while I get it ready. Then (*Gloria's idea of a Southern accent*) we're "jist gonna laze around all day and brunch out."

GRACE: Roy stopped in this mornin'. Little after sun-up. Come to talk about— Well, if I had any idea how long it might take me. You know, to— "pass on?"

GLORIA: He asked you that?

GRACE: Seems he's got tickets to a stock car race down in Florida. I told him, "Roy, honey," I said, "I'm dying fast as I can."

GLORIA: That creep! What's wrong with him?

GRACE: He's young. Wants to bust loose. Nothin' much left anymore to keep him here.

GLORIA: I wouldn't be too sure about that. Peter and I spent an hour this morning with your "Apple Glade" developer. Oh Grace, it was so wonderful. The guy's exactly how you'd picture him. A real sleaze. Pudgy, sweaty. He didn't talk, he growled. Vowed he was going to sue us if we delayed his project one more day. I told him that was interesting, because we were planning a suit of our own.

GRACE: We're planning what?

GLORIA: Peter was surprised, too. You see, I stopped at my realtor's office this morning and had her do some checking. She discovered that when you sold this farm you were, not swindled exactly, but at least taken advantage of. It's my guess the people at your bank were so anxious to impress this developer, they scared you into selling the farm for a lot less than it was worth. Me, I think we should sue the bank, too.

GRACE: I want you to stop this. Stop it right now!

GLORIA: But you were cheated!

GRACE: I don't care! Lawsuits. Now you got me dyin' in some courtroom!

GLORIA: No one's going to court. Give me a few more sessions with that sleazebag developer and I guarantee he'll come around to a nice, quiet settlement.

GRACE: And what does that mean?

GLORIA: It means the difference between what the land was worth and what you sold it for. The realtor wants to check into it more, but she's sure we're talking a hundred thousand minimum.

GRACE: A hundred thousand dollars?

GLORIA: You sold five hundred acres, Grace.

GRACE: But a hundred thousand dollars?

GLORIA: That's the upside. The downside is it's going to take time. And that's what your will is for. Here, (*Going to her bag*) I had Peter give me a standard form. All we have to do is fill in a few blanks.

GRACE: And just who'm I supposed to leave it to?

GLORIA: Anyone you want. Roy.

GRACE: Why would I leave it to Roy?

GLORIA (*Setting the will form in front of Grace*): You said he was disappointed he didn't have an inheritance. Now, maybe he'll remember you differently.

GRACE: I'm supposed to buy Roy's fond memories of me?

GLORIA: Forget Roy. Leave it to— a church.

GRACE: Told you, I don't have a church.

GLORIA: Yes, you did. How about— Luanne?

GRACE: Luanne? What would she do with all that money?

GLORIA: Set up a trust to pay for her college education. By the time Luanne's old enough for college it's going to cost a hundred thou.

GRACE: Her Mamma's divorced, got two other kids.

GLORIA: Then that's it. We'll set up a trust. Oh Grace, this is beautiful. I mean it, it's so beautiful.

GRACE: 'Course you know what the Bible says about money. The root of all evil. Buys nothing but misery. I don't believe I want that on my conscience.

GLORIA: Grace, this isn't the same.

GRACE (*tearing up the will form*):   We will forget about this!

GLORIA: Grace!

GRACE (*throwing the paper down*):   NO!

GLORIA: Fine.

GRACE: I don't like what's happenin' to me. I'm so confused. Ever since last night, my mind is—

GLORIA: I told you I was sorry about last night.

GRACE: Ain't sayin' I'm doubtin'. Never doubted the good Lord one second o' my life. But you got me wonderin'. So many things. Like I was listenin' to my music this mornin', but I was hearin' it different somehow. "Gladly will I toil and suffer, only let me walk with Thee." I don't like sayin' this, but, try as I might, I was never glad about the toilin' *or* the sufferin'.

(*Gloria sets a beautifully arranged tray, complete with a tea rose in a bud vase, on the table*)

GLORIA: Well, there'll be no "toilin' or sufferin'" today. Ta-da!

GRACE: Now why did you go and buy all this food? One thing we got plenty of 'round here is food.

GLORIA: This food is special. To me, anyway. This is the city, Grace. I thought maybe you'd like to . . . Here, try this.

GRACE: What is it?

GLORIA: It's called prosciutto. On a sliver of raisin pumpernickel.

GRACE: Pro what?

GLORIA: It's a kind of ham. Taste it.

GRACE: What kind of ham?

GLORIA: It's Italian.

GRACE: *I*-talian ham? Don't smell like no ham I ever ate. Fact, smells like it's gone bad.

GLORIA: It hasn't gone bad. Just taste it. It's meat.

GRACE: You wanted meat why didn't you say so? We could've gone out back and killed us one of them chickens.

GLORIA: Grace, please.

GRACE: You don't eat chicken?

GLORIA: Not ones I've made eye-contact with!

GRACE: Least it'd be fresh killed. Not like that stuff there. You ask me that pro-shoo-to's been dead a long time.

GLORIA: Okay, forget the meat. Try this. It's called brie— It's— cheese.

GRACE: Cheese? Why would you buy cheese? I got a whole carton of Velveeta in the ice box.

GLORIA: Just smell it, Grace. (*Gloria takes a whiff*) Isn't that heaven?

GRACE (*taking a little sniff*): I sure hope not. (*Gloria throws down the brie*) What's that stuff?

GLORIA: I'm not telling you!

GRACE: What is it?

GLORIA: It's lobster salad. Look, I'm eating it. Mmmm!

GRACE: I seen pictures of lobsters. All them legs and them beady little eyes. They look like giant—

GLORIA: Don't say it, Grace. I'm warning you!

GRACE: "Cockroach" bugs!

GLORIA (*jumping up*): OKAY, FORGET IT! FORGET THE FOOD, FORGET THE MONEY, FORGET EVERYTHING! Peter's always saying I'm an over-achiever, maybe he's right!

GRACE: Listen, honey, you want to eat that stuff, don't let me stop you.

GLORIA: I seem to have lost my appetite!

GRACE (*going to the refrigerator*): Can't say as I blame you. How about I fix us both a nice Velveeta cheese sandwich?

GLORIA: Sit down, Grace. I'll make you a sandwich.

GRACE: Use that Wonder bread there. It's still fresh. And put some of this Miracle Whip on it.

GLORIA: Miracle Whip and Velveeta on Wonder. Why didn't I think of that?

GRACE (*sitting down, noticing the lobster salad*): What you should've done is stayed home and fixed your husband his dinner. (*She wants a taste but doesn't have the nerve*) What on earth is the poor man doin' without you?

GLORIA (*at the counter fixing the sandwich*): The poor man is having the time of his life. (*Grace picks up a small piece of lobster, smells it*) This afternoon he's over at his partner's house watching college football. (*Grace pops the meat into her mouth. She starts to chew*) What I don't understand, before we moved here? (*Gloria turns. Grace freezes*) You all right? (*Grace nods. Gloria turns back to*

73

the sandwich. Grace chews) Peter wouldn't be caught dead watching televised sports. But now. I don't know what's happening to him. It's football and beer and— You know lately he comes home from work and goes straight for his old levis and flannel shirt. And this green baseball cap with "John Deere" written on it. (*Gloria turns. Sees Grace helping herself to another morsel. The old bat! Gloria turns back to the sandwich*) In New York this same man would put on a three piece suit and tie to go out and walk the dog.

GRACE: Maybe he's just tryin' to fit in.

GLORIA: Oh, he's fitting in all right. He's turning into a back-woods, redneck right before my eyes. Now he's talking about buying a four-by-four pick-up truck.

GRACE: Like the one Roy drives?

GLORIA: Yes. Oh, I hope you don't think— I didn't mean that everyone who drives a pick-up truck is a—

GRACE: A redneck? Roy *is* a redneck. So am I. A back-woods redneck to boot.

GLORIA: Okay, I'm sorry. I don't know what happens. Sometimes I can be such a—

GRACE: Snob's a good word.

GLORIA: Would you like me to take that away, or should I wait until you're finished with it?

GRACE: I don't know what you mean. (*Gloria wipes Grace's mouth with a napkin*) Okay, I tasted it, your "New York" lobster. That's what you wanted, ain't it?

GLORIA: Good wasn't it?

GRACE: Like chewing an old tractor tire!

GLORIA: I'll bet! Here's your sandwich.

GRACE: Now *that* looks good. But where's yours?

GLORIA: I told you, I lost my appe—

GRACE: I can't eat this whole thing. Here, you eat half.

GLORIA: No, Grace, I mean it. I'm not—

GRACE (*taunting*): I'm just askin' you to *taste* it. (*They bite simultaneously*) Good, huh?

GLORIA (*prying the gummy bread and cheese from the roof of her mouth*): Mmmm.

GRACE: Maybe your husband's decided to relax and enjoy himself. That happens to Yankees when they move down here. They slow down. Lift their nose off the grindstone and smell the honeysuckle. Wouldn't hurt you to give it a try.

GLORIA: Grace I don't want to be a redneck! I want to go to the opera, art museums. I want to eat in a restaurant that doesn't have wagon wheel lanterns hanging from the ceiling!

GRACE: Just look out at them mountains. At the colors of them trees. Ain't been an artist ever lived could paint a picture pretty as that. (*She puts down the rest of her sandwich*) I'll have to save the rest of this for later. I'm full.

GLORIA: But you only took one bite.

GRACE (*standing, going to the sink*): I know.

GLORIA: Come to think of it, I'm full, too.

GRACE: Oh, no. You said you was hungry. You finish that. No one goes hungry in my house.

GLORIA: What are you doing?

GRACE: Thought I'd peel these apples. (*Finding a slip of paper on the counter*) Oh, and here. I had Roy write out Luanne's address. You know, for the sweater?

GLORIA (*hurrying to her things*): Luanne's sweater! I almost forgot! Oh, Grace, I had this spectacular idea! Remember how you said you always wanted to write to Luanne, tell her about yourself. On the way home it came to me. A way for that to happen.

GRACE (*peeling apples*): You goin' to teach me how to write before I die? You are an over-achiever.

GLORIA: Look at this. (*She takes a mini-cam out of the bag*) Know what this is? It's a video camera. It takes pictures. TV pictures. And it records them on—

GRACE: I don't care what it is. What's it got to do with me and Luanne?

GLORIA: I'm going to make a tape of you. To send to Luanne. And while she's trying on her apple orchard sweater, she'll actually be able to see *you* on TV wishing *her* a happy birthday! How about it? Isn't that a terrific idea?

GRACE: I don't think so.

GLORIA: But she'll finally see this "amazing" aunt she's been writing to all these years. See you and hear you. Think of how thrilled she'll be. It'll be something she can keep for the rest of her life!

GRACE: Glorie, I mean it. I'm—

GLORIA: Oh, and Peter suggested—and I agree—that as long as we're making tapes, it would be helpful if we could record, in some detail, how you'd like your estate settled. That way we'll have a video attesting to the authenticity of your will.

GRACE: What will?

GLORIA: Oh. I mean, of course—

GRACE: I tore up that will!

GLORIA: That was just a form, Grace, I have others.

GRACE: You just can't take no for an answer, can you?

GLORIA: Grace—

GRACE: It's not bad enough you put on airs, YOU'RE ALSO SPOILT!

GLORIA: Oh. Is that right?

GRACE: And now you're hurt.

GLORIA (*putting the camera away*): Damn right I'm hurt.

GRACE: What do you expect? You come stormin' in here with your fancy foods, your wills, your talk of thousands and thousands of dollars, your TV tapes, and you expect me to be grateful? I'm an old woman. I'm set in my ways. Can't you understand that?

GLORIA (*clearing up the brunch things*): I'm sorry.

GRACE: I don't like surprises. That's why I got upset.

GLORIA: I understand.

GRACE: I didn't mean to hurt you.

GLORIA: Let's just forget it.

GRACE: Yes. Fine. (*The two women are quiet a moment. Gloria works in the kitchen. Grace peels apples*) That TV machine. Shows what a person really looks like, don't it?

GLORIA: It's very accurate. Yes.

GRACE: Well, there's another reason.

GLORIA: Grace, you look fine. You're beautiful.

GRACE: Beautiful? I look like something on the highway. What's Roy call it? "Road kill!"

GLORIA: We do up your hair. Put on a little make-up.

GRACE: Don't use make-up. Never have.

GLORIA: A little lipstick. A light blush. How can it hurt?

GRACE: A painted woman. That's what you want me to show Luanne?

GLORIA: No, of course not. Can we just forget about this?

(*A moment*)

GRACE: You got make-up on now?

GLORIA: See, you can't even tell.

GRACE: Woman wears that stuff makes you wonder what's she tryin' to hide.

GLORIA: Make-up isn't meant to hide things, it's meant to accent, to highlight the beauty that's already there.

GRACE: You sound like an ad on TV.

GLORIA: Give me five minutes, Grace. Five minutes with my make-up kit—

GRACE: No, I won't let you talk me into this.

GLORIA: You're the one that's talking you into it, not me.

GRACE: Even if by some miracle you could make me look half-way presentable, what would I say to her? To Luanne?

GLORIA: Wish her a happy birthday.

GRACE: I can do that with a Hallmark card.

GLORIA: Then tell her . . . tell her something she can use, something you've learned in your life.

GRACE: And just what have I learned in my life? You said it yourself. My life's been for nothin'!

GLORIA: Grace!

GRACE: Absolutely nothin'! I'm an illiterate, backwards old woman!

GLORIA: DAMNIT, GRACE!

(A *Bulldozer* starts up with an explosive roar. The two women stop. Another Bulldozer roars to life)

GRACE: Someone's startin' them machines.

GLORIA (*running to the window*):   But they can't. There's a court order.

GRACE: What are they doing? Well?

GLORIA: Two men. They seem to be—

GRACE: What?

GLORIA: They're on the bulldozers. They seem to be heading for—

GRACE (*getting up*): Heading for what?

GLORIA: Oh my god.

(*There is a loud crack followed by a crash*)

GRACE: The orchard!

GLORIA: I'm calling the sheriff.

(*Another loud crash. Grace hurries out the door. Gloria bangs on the phone*)

GLORIA: I can't get a dial tone. Those bastards must have cut— (*Another loud crash. Gloria turns*) Grace? (*Gloria sees the door open.*) GRACE!

GRACE (*off*): STOP! STOP IT! STOP IT!

GLORIA (*running out the door*): Grace! Come back! GRACE!

(*As the lights fade the roar of the machinery swells with the cracking and falling of old apple trees*)

BLACKOUT

(*End of Scene 1.*)

Scene 2

Early that evening; a cold wind is blowing. Grace is in bed.
Gloria is spreading another quilt over her.

GLORIA: There. Does that feel warmer?

GRACE: Will you stop fussin' over me?

GLORIA: You said you were cold.

GRACE: I've been cold before.

GLORIA: I'll put another stick on the fire. Then we'll have
a nice cup of tea.

GRACE: I don't want no tea.

GLORIA: But you're shivering.

GRACE: I'm shiverin' 'cause I'm mad, not 'cause I'm cold!
You think I'm a fool, don't you? Carrying on like this over
a few old trees.

GLORIA: They had sentimental value. I understand.

GRACE: They had more than sentimental value! They
were majestic, old trees! (*A moment*) I'm sorry. I'm tired.

GLORIA: Why don't you take a nap?

GRACE: You're just trying to get rid of me. (*Gloria gives
up. Sits. Another moment*) You got something to do?

GLORIA (*startled*): Yes, of course, I'm . . . (*She looks around. Goes to the table*) I should gather up these things from Hospice.

GRACE: I kept askin' myself, why the orchard? What'd those trees ever do 'cept give beauty, food, comfort. (*Gloria gets her attache case*) Then it come to me. That developer from Northern Virginia. He was sending me a message. That's what it was, and you know it. You and your lawsuits. But they needed them trees. For the name. Who'm I kiddin'. Names don't mean nothing no more. "Apple Glade." Sounds like somethin' comes in a spray can.

GLORIA: Okay, so it was a reprisal. We made the sleazebag mad. In business you try to make your adversary mad so he'll do stupid things. And what this guy did today was really stupid. I just hope you don't let him get away with it.

GRACE: I suppose we're back to lawsuits again.

GLORIA: You said it yourself, Grace, no one's going to know you ever even lived. This is your chance to change that. To let everyone know you not only lived, but that your life had some value!

GRACE: Is that how I give my life value, by leavin' behind a pile o' money?!

GLORIA: I'm not talking just about money, I'm talking— Grace, you have a chance here to give Luanne all the things you never had. Education, opportunity. And freedom, Grace. Freedom to grow and blossom as she pleases. And all you'll have to do is—

GRACE: NO! NO MORE! Honey I got to ask you a big favor. Please stop helpin' me.

(*Gloria sits, picks up a pamphlet and reads. A moment passes*)

GRACE: What's that you're reading?

GLORIA: I thought you were going to take a nap.

GRACE: You thought wrong. What're you readin'?

GLORIA: Just something from Hospice.

GRACE: That tell you how to handle a sentimental old woman?

GLORIA: No.

GRACE: What's it say?

GLORIA: It's not important.

GRACE: If it's not important why'd they write it down? What's it say?

GLORIA: Grace, take your nap, please.

GRACE: Read it to me.

GLORIA: I'm not reading this to you.

GRACE: It might make me fall asleep.

GLORIA: I'll find something else. Your Bible. I'll read from your Bible.

GRACE: I don't want to hear the Bible. What's it about?

GLORIA: Grace.

GRACE: What's it about!

GLORIA: It's about— If you must know, it's called "The Signs and Symptoms of Approaching—"

GRACE: Death.

GLORIA: I just picked this up. It doesn't mean anything. I was looking for something to do!

GRACE: Read it.

GLORIA: Please, Grace.

GRACE: What are the signs and symptoms?

GLORIA: Why are you doing this?

GRACE: Don't I got a right to know what to expect?

GLORIA: Yes. You have a right.

GRACE: Then read it. Well? Listen, Glorie, you're not goin' to shock me. If there's one thing I know about—

85

GLORIA: It's death. Yes, you told me. All right! "The Signs and Symptoms of Approaching *Death!*"

GRACE: Go on.

GLORIA: Grace.

GRACE: Go on!

GLORIA: "The arms and legs of the body may become cool to the touch. You may notice the underside of the body becoming darker in color. These symptoms are a result of blood circulation slowing down."

GRACE: That happened to Roger Lee. He got all cold.

GLORIA: "The patient will gradually spend more time sleeping and at times will be difficult to arouse. This symptom is a result of a change in the body's metabolism. The patient's vision may begin to fail. As will the hearing. Saliva may gather in the back of the throat. This causes a rasping sound when the patient breathes. This sound is commonly called—"

GRACE: Death rattle. That's what it's called. Death rattle.

GLORIA: Yes.

GRACE: Keep readin'.

GLORIA: "The patient may become increasingly confused about time, place, the identity of close and familiar people."

GRACE: Confused. Yes, yes, I know about that. You start wonderin' things.

GLORIA: Grace.

GRACE: Things you never wondered about in your whole life. Like why God even bothered to put you on this earth! (*Sitting up*) Let's do it! Get your make-up things! Paint my face!

GLORIA: What?

GRACE: Get your make-up! I want you to doll me up!

GLORIA: Now?

GRACE: I want to talk to Luanne.

GLORIA: Luanne? Are you sure?

GRACE: I don't believe this! You've been driving me crazy all day and when I finally agree— (*Getting out of bed*) Where do you want me? Should I sit at the table?

GLORIA (*pulling out a chair*): No, here.

GRACE: This is vanity. You know that, don't you? The vice of vanity!

GLORIA: Relax, Grace. When a woman hits thirty, vanity becomes a virtue.

GRACE: A virtue. Yes. I'll tell that to Eve when I see her.

GLORIA: Eve?

GRACE (*sitting*): It's because of Eve's vanity women suffer like we do. Because she give in to the devil, ate the forbidden fruit. That's why women wear make-up. To hide their shame.

GLORIA: Oh, right. First the apple then Revlon.

GRACE: You don't believe in the story of Adam and Eve?

GLORIA (*assembling the make-up*): Oh, no. You're not sucking me into this.

GRACE: You probably don't believe in the Bible neither.

GLORIA: Hold still.

GRACE: You ever read the Bible?

GLORIA: Yes, I've read the Bible. I was raised a God-fearing, church-going, money-loving Episcopalian.

GRACE: And what happened? When did you stop believin'?

GLORIA: Turn your head.

GRACE: You won't answer because you know in your heart that the "Good Book" is true. Ain't that right? (*Gloria is straining to be quiet*) Just 'cause I can't read it don't mean I don't know it's true.

GLORIA: You're a liberated thinker, Grace. Did you ever ask yourself who wrote this "Good Book?"

GRACE: There were many men that—

GLORIA: Men! That's the operative word. Men wrote the "Good Book." Every word of it.

GRACE: But all of them were holy men. Like the story of Adam and Eve. Moses himself wrote that part.

GLORIA: You think Moses was going to blame mankind's first sin on another member of the great fraternity? Here, hold this.

GRACE: Eve was the weaker of the two. Our old minister at church told us that one Sunday. The Serpent tempted Eve to eat the forbidden fruit because she was the weaker. 'Course I do remember thinkin' at the time—

GLORIA: What?

GRACE: Well, men are stronger than women, got bigger muscles and all, but when it comes to temptation—

GLORIA: Yes?

GRACE: Men are pretty easy.

GLORIA: They are indeed! Now if the Bible were written for women—

GRACE: There's women in the Bible, lots of 'em.

GLORIA: Wives, mistresses, whores, and slaves! You know there're many of us, Grace, who've believed for quite some time now, that if there is a God, she's a woman.

GRACE: That's a hot one! God's a woman. I worry about your soul, honey.

GLORIA: And this business of Eve and the "forbidden fruit." So she cost us our cushy berth in paradise, look at all she gave us. Yearning, passion, satisfaction, poetry.

GRACE: She also give us death. (*This sobers Gloria. A beat*) What are you doing now?

GLORIA: Softening your cheek bones.

GRACE: Good. Always hated my cheekbones.

GLORIA: Close your eyes.

GRACE: Do you talk to your husband this way?

GLORIA: What way?

GRACE: This liberated woman kind of talk?

GLORIA: Sure. All the time.

GRACE: And he lets you get away with it?

GLORIA: He doesn't have much choice.

GRACE: I'd ever talked to Mr. Stiles that way, he'd o' hauled off and hit me with a fence post.

GLORIA: Okay, now hold your head really still.

GRACE: What for?

GLORIA: Mascara. No, don't blink. Concentrate, damnit.

GRACE: You have such a foul mouth.

GLORIA: You sound like my husband.

GRACE: He don't like your foul mouth neither?

GLORIA: There's a lot about me he doesn't like.

GRACE: Does he—you know, blame you for what happened to your little boy?

GLORIA: He blames it on the way we were living. (*Digging in her bag for the right lipstick*) In New York. Fast, intense, expensive. Both of us, we were working twelve, fourteen hours a day. I told you Peter hated the city, but for me— Open your mouth. (*She applies lipstick*) My job, it wasn't like work. You get into this rhythm, this pace. The city does that to you. There's so "much." In a way that was *my* orchard, Grace. It's where I dreamt *my* dreams. I promised myself when I got married that I could handle being a wife, a mother, and still have a career. And I did, too. And then when I met this— hunk of a guy, it was—

GRACE: Was what?

GLORIA: Don't talk. It was fabulous. Here, blot your lips. (*Showing Grace how to blot her lips, she sits on the edge of the bed*) I know you couldn't possibly understand, Grace, but the pressure of my job, the tension. I needed someone, I don't know, someone to— You see, Peter never expected me to succeed, and when I not only succeeded but passed him in the process— Well, we came this close to splitting up. We would have, too— if it weren't for the accident. For Danny. What happened to my life, Grace? I mean no one believed in herself more. Did I want too much? Like our sister, Eve, did I bite into some forbidden fruit?

GRACE: You young people, all talkin' 'bout "believin' in yourself." I always thought faith was believin' in somethin' bigger. Listen, Glorie, I ain't sitting here gettin' younger. We 'bout done?

GLORIA: Except for your hair. What'll we do with your hair?

GRACE: We could throw one of these quilts over it.

GLORIA (*digging through her cosmetic bag*):   We need something original. Here we go. (*She squirts some mousse into her hand*)

GRACE: What's that stuff? Looks like whipped-up egg whites.

GLORIA: You know, I think it is.

GRACE: Well, that's original, all right. If I lived fifty more years, I never would o' thought of wearing a meringue.

GLORIA (*working the foam into Grace's hair*): It's called mousse. I use it all the time.

(*Grace relaxes, revels in having her scalp rubbed*)

GRACE: He was a preacher.

GLORIA: Who was?

GRACE: A temporary preacher.

GLORIA: Who are we talking about?

GRACE (*mocking*): "I couldn't possibly understand." You think only you civilized people got them kind o' feelin's?

GLORIA: Oh, you mean . . . Oh!

GRACE: He was a young man. Come in one summer when our old preacher got sick. I was married, o' course. Had three, four kids by then.

GLORIA: This young preacher, was he handsome?

GRACE: Oh, boy.

GLORIA: Did he make you feel all— you know.

GRACE: Like a lump o' lard in a hot skillet! Only man in my whole life ever said out loud I was pretty.

GLORIA: Oh, Grace. That's so sweet.

GRACE: Wasn't sweet at all. One mornin' in Sunday School he asked me to stand up'n read something from the Bible. Everybody in the room started to laugh. They all knew I couldn't read. I was so ashamed. Afterwards he come up to me. Told me not to feel bad. Said he'd teach me. Poor man. I'd go over to the church Saturday afternoons, sit there in front o' him with this book. But I couldn't concentrate. I kept lookin' at him. Watchin' his eyes, the funny way he'd wrinkle his brow whenever I made a mistake. Listenin' to him laugh. The people in church, my mother-in-law especially, pretty soon they started cacklin' like a flock of old hens. Didn't take long for my husband to find out. He stormed down to that church and made 'em send that preacher packin'. Things was never great with Mr. Stiles before that summer. I won't tell you how it was after.

GLORIA: But why? Did anything happen?

GRACE: 'Course nothin' happened!

GLORIA (*getting a tea rose from the bud vase*): Now don't get upset.

GRACE: I was so angry after that. With all of 'em. The people at church, Gabriella, my husband, even with— I know I told you I never doubted God. That ain't exactly true.

GLORIA: That was a long time ago. Hold still.

GRACE: Hold still! I'm rememberin' things goin' to send me to hell for all eternity and you tell me to hold still!

GLORIA (*putting the rose in Grace's hair*):   There. (*She steps back, admiring her work*) Oh, yes.

GRACE: What?

GLORIA (*hurrying to the dresser*):   I'm going to get a mirror. Now you sit there and don't move. Don't even breathe. (*Grace slowly lifts her hands to her face*) Don't touch! (*Gloria returns with the mirror*) Okay, are you ready?

GRACE: I don't think I want to look. (*Gloria goes behind Grace. Holds out the mirror. Grace slowly turns. Her eyes widen*) That young preacher man was right.

GLORIA (*starting to take the mirror away*):   Are you ready to talk to Luanne now?

GRACE: Don't take the mirror. (*Gazing at herself*) Oh, how I wish—

(*Grace freezes. Takes a quick breath. Her face goes blank*)

GLORIA: Grace? Grace, what is it?

GRACE: Pain.

GLORIA: Oh, god.

GRACE: Goin' to be bad.

GLORIA: Grace?

GRACE: Oh, sweet Jesus.

GLORIA (*reaching for the morphine*):   Listen to me.

GRACE: Sweet Jesus.

GLORIA: Grace, this is morphine. You know how to use—

GRACE: NO! NO DRUGS!

GLORIA: BUT YOU CAN'T SURVIVE ANOTHER ONE OF THESE! IT WILL KILL YOU!

GRACE: Oh, sweet Jesus!

GLORIA: DAMNIT, GRACE! THERE IS NO REASON TO SUFFER LIKE THIS!

GRACE: I DON'T CARE! WON'T DO NO GOOD! (*Gloria holds Grace's mouth open, administers the drops. Grace pulls away*) The signs! The signs o' death comin'. Bet you can see 'em already! How many times have I seen 'em. You get restless; you pull at the bed clothes. You start havin' visions, crazy visions! Visions of God! Oh, but if I see God, he won't be there, will he? Bernice said only fools believe in God. That what I am? A FOOL! When my little Carroll died. When I was holdin' on to Duane and his blood was pumpin' out of that bullet hole and I prayed for God to make the bleedin' stop, prayed to let my baby live. WAS I JUST TALKIN' TO THE AIR? That why my babies died? CAUSE THERE WAS NO GOD TO SAVE 'EM? All the times I was cold and hungry and hurtin' and wantin' to run away from this miserable farm. But I thought this is where God wanted me to be. Now you tell me I could o' gone? Could o' gone to Richmond or Atlanta. Could o' found me a man with a little joy in him. A man who would o' loved me, said out loud I was pretty! Is that what you come here for? (*Shouting*) TO TELL ME MY WHOLE LIFE WAS FOR NOTHIN'?!

GLORIA: Grace, please.

GRACE: And when I close my eyes for the last time will that be it? GRACE STILES WILL BE NO MORE?

GLORIA: Please listen to—

GRACE: Honey, I know I'm ignorant, but like your Mamma, I've been happy in my ignorance! WHY COULDN'T YOU O' JUST LET ME DIE THAT WAY? WHAT ARE YOU DOIN' JUST STANDING THERE! I DON'T WANT YOU HERE! GET OUT!

GLORIA: Grace.

GRACE: GO HOME! GIVE ME A FEW MINUTES OF PEACE BEFORE I DIE! AND TAKE THOSE THINGS WITH YOU! THAT FANCY FOOD! THAT CAMERA. ALL OF IT! I WANT IT OUT OF HERE! I'm an old woman. Why can't you understand that? I'm set in my ways. I've always been set in my ways. What are you waiting for? Go on, get out of here!

GLORIA: I can't.

GRACE: Told you, I don't need you!

GLORIA: Yes you do! Just as I need you. Grace, I'll proba-bly never believe in the same things you do. But in the last few days, you've shown me . . . that it might be possible to believe in something again. I keep thinking about your niece. I don't even know Luanne but I feel connected to her somehow. Isn't it possible she's searching for something, too? Why else would she have wanted to come all this way to visit you? If not to learn firsthand the secrets her great, great aunt has to share. Are you listening to me? Grace? Grace.

GRACE (*a little surprised*):   Pain's goin' away.

GLORIA: Yes.

GRACE: It's that morphine, ain't it?

GLORIA: Yes.

(*Grace stands. She's unsteady. Gloria hurries to her. Helps her into bed*)

GRACE: How do I look? Did I mess up my face?

GLORIA: You look fine.

GRACE: My hair? It's still all right?

GLORIA: Yes, yes, it's fine.

GRACE: Then we might as well get this over with. Go on, get that TV camera.

GLORIA: You're sure?

GRACE: You think I'm goin' through this "mascara and mousse" again, you got another think comin'!

GLORIA: Grace, thank you. Thank you. (*Setting up the tripod*)

GRACE: 'Course I don't have the faintest idea—

GLORIA: Don't worry, you're going to be wonderful. Now just hang on, this will only take a sec.

GRACE: You sure I look okay?

GLORIA: Like a movie star.

GRACE: Ha! Is it light enough in here?

GLORIA: Yes.

GRACE: Look at me, I'm all jittery.

GLORIA: Now just try to relax. Think about what you want to say. As soon as I'm ready just look up here at the camera. Pretend you're talking to Luanne.

GRACE: I can't pretend a machine's a person.

GLORIA: Then look at me. Pretend I'm Luanne. Okay, all set? No, look up at me. Here we go.

GRACE: All right? (*Gloria nods, starts the camera. Grace is stiff, nervous. She shouts*) LUANNE! (*Gloria motions to her speak softer*) I'm s'posed to talk normal? (*Gloria nods, waves at her to continue*) Luanne? (*She blanks*) I can't think of nothin' to say.

GLORIA (*stopping the camera*):   Okay. We can start over. Just relax. Wish Luanne a happy birthday. And—what? Here. Show her the sweater.

GRACE: She can see this?

GLORIA: Sure. Ready?

GRACE (*looking at the camera. Still stiff*):   Luanne? Hi. This is me. Your great aunt. Grace. I . . . Oh, yes. Happy birthday. I . . . I wanted to let you know how much your letters've meant to me. And the pictures you sent me. Sure loved them pictures. Can't believe you're a teenager already. I'm glad you been thinkin' 'bout me. I been thinkin' 'bout you, too, all the while I been . . . (*She's relaxing now. Talking to Luanne*) knittin' this sweater. See? It's a picture of an old orchard used to be out there on a hill. Thought you might like to see it. Wish I could see *you*. Give you a hug. Hope you're not too big for hugs. (*A beat*) This is . . . probably the only chance I'm goin' to get to talk to you. S'pose I should be givin' you advice. People expect ol' folks to do that. Give 'em advice. But you young women today, you're so bright, so independent, what can I tell you? Don't even know myself what I know. This little farm here: the animals, the trees, the flowers, the . . . bugs. It's been my whole world. It's like— (*She fidgets with the sweater uncomfortably*) Maybe . . . (*She begins to get excited*) maybe it's like this . . . like this sweater. I mean the way everythin' in this whole world is, you know, connected. Like the stitches in this sweater. See, each one, they ain't much by themselves, but you break even one and the whole sweater falls apart. Now I might not know what my life's been for, Luanne, but I do know God put me here on this earth for a reason.

Even if it was only, like a stitch in the middle of this sweater, to hold on with one hand to the stitch that comes before me and with the other hand to the stitch that comes after. If that's all I was put here to do, it's still a mighty important thing. And it makes me a mighty important person. (*She's looking at Gloria*) I think that's all God wants any of us to do, honey. Hold on. To each other and to this sweet earth He give us with all our might. Guess that's 'bout all I got to say. (*Tears are running down her cheeks*) Give Mommy a hug from me. Will you do that? I love you, sweetheart. I love you.

GLORIA: Amen.

GRACE: Look at me, cryin' like a baby! And that black stuff on my eyes? Probably leakin' all down my face. Why, I bet I look just like that . . . that Tammy Faye Baker on TV!

GLORIA (*laughing*): You do. You look just like Tammy Faye.

(*Gloria gets a tissue. Cleans Grace's face*)

GRACE: I wasn't talking only to Luanne, you know.

GLORIA: Yes, I know.

GRACE: I'm cold.

GLORIA: Here, lie back. Let me pull up the covers.

GRACE: Feel my legs. They feel cold to you?

GLORIA: No.

GRACE: They don't feel cold?

GLORIA: You're warmer than I am.

GRACE: Then you don't think I'm dyin' just yet?

GLORIA: No. You're not dying just yet.

GRACE: If I take a nap you think I'll wake up?

GLORIA: You haven't finished Luanne's sweater.

GRACE: I do have this little bit to finish around the neck. Okay, I'll . . . take a nap.

GLORIA: And when you wake up, we'll work on your will.

GRACE: You and that will! All right, yes, we'll work on my will! I mean I don't know how you're going to squeeze any money out of that—wha'ja call him?—that "sleazebag" from up north, but there's not a doubt in my mind you're goin' to do it!

GLORIA: I don't suppose you've thought about how you'd like the money used.

GRACE: What's to think about? I want half of it to go to Roy. I know, I know, but he is my closest next of kin.

GLORIA: And the rest?

GRACE: That's for Luanne, of course. For her college. I *would* like her to have some o' the things I never had. 'Specially the— How'd you say it? Freedom to grow and blossom? Oh, and I want to leave something to you.

GLORIA: Don't be silly. You know I shouldn't have even come here.

GRACE: You're not sorry you did.

GLORIA: Oh, no. Now, is there anything else? I mean, anything you'd like to add to your will?

GRACE: Not that I can think of. Why we talkin' 'bout this now?

GLORIA (*going to the video camera*): Grace, I told you, we needed something to help authenticate your will.

GRACE: You mean that thing's been runnin' all the while I've been lyin' here jabberin'?

GLORIA (*turning off the camera*): Say good night, Grace.

GRACE (*turning away*): Well ain't you somethin'!

GLORIA: Please don't be angry with me.

GRACE: Oh, I ain't angry. Just a little wore out trying to keep up with you. I mean, let's face it. You're pretty amazin' yourself. (*Gloria's eyes fill with tears*) Now don't you forget. Half hour, that's all. Oh, and if you see Death comin' . . .

GLORIA: I will. I'll wake you.

GRACE: You cryin', honey?

GLORIA: Yes.

GRACE: Why?

GLORIA: I don't know.

GRACE (*holding out her hand*):   Maybe you're grievin' for me already.

GLORIA (*taking Grace's hand, sitting on the bed*):   Maybe so.

GRACE: Them other people you helped die. You grieve for them, too?

GLORIA: I guess I did.

GRACE: That's what this is, this messin' with death you do. You think if you stop grievin' you'll finally have to let go of your little boy.

GLORIA: I loved him so much, Grace.

GRACE: 'Course you did. But, honey, it wasn't death tied you and that little boy together, it was life. That's what "our sister Eve" give us when she bit that apple. All the glory o' life.

(*Gloria nods. Grace closes her eyes. Gloria releases Grace's hand, leans back, sits there lost in thought. It's quiet for a long moment*)

GRACE (*without opening her eyes*):   You got something to do?

GLORIA (*jumping up, startled, exasperated*):   Yes, Grace, I've got something to do!

GRACE (*laughing*):   I know what I'll leave you! I want you to put this in my will. I want you to have "Gabriella's soup tureen!" What do you say to that?

GLORIA (*laughing*):   Grace, I would be honored.

GRACE: Really? (*She reaches out her hand. Gloria holds it*) I'm so glad. 'Cause then you'll be able to remember for the rest of your life what an ornery, old "piss-pot" I've been!

(*Grace closes her eyes and falls asleep. Gloria kisses the old woman's hand then tucks it under the quilt. She is about to sit, but catches herself. She stands, looks around. She crosses to the sink, picks up a knife and a bright red apple. She is about to start peeling the apple but stops. She looks briefly at Grace, looks back at the apple. Then takes a huge noisy bite as the lights fade out*)

END OF PLAY